Spirit Crossfire

Books by Stephen L. Thompson

The Crossfire Series

Colorado Crossfire
International Crossfire
Israeli Crossfire
Believer's Crossfire
Spirit Crossfire
Faith Crossfire
Chinese Crossfire
Texas Crossfire
Dark Crossfire
Island Crossfire
Jagged Crossfire
Violent Crossfire
Russian Crossfire
Nuclear Crossfire
End Times Crossfire
Revelation Crossfire
Gates of Hell Crossfire
Assassin's Crossfire
Albatross Crossfire
Global Crossfire
Far East Crossfire

The SFO Series

Station Force One - Onset

Spirit Crossfire

The Enemy Counter-Attacks

Stephen L. Thompson

Spirit Crossfire

The Crossfire Team battles with unknown enemies launching attacks against the team's members. A reclusive billionaire invites the Malones to his island in the Pacific Ocean. There the team discovers an evil plan set to destroy the nation of Israel.

As the team centers their sights on a mysterious group known as the NIL, they make a horrible discovery. The NIL have developed an air-borne poison that they believe will kill all of their enemy's children. Satan plans to use these vermin to eliminate all children in the world.

As the action races to a climax, part of the team is captured by a demonic force that desires to harm them violently.

-   Stephen L. Thompson

Spirit Crossfire

Published by
Stephen L. Thompson
Facebook.com/CrossfireNovelSeries

ISBN- 978-0-9850758-9-7

Published in the United States of America

Foreword

To my Christian readers –

The Crossfire series of action/adventure stories include depictions of violence which are unusual in Christian literature. It would be nice if there were no conflict or violence in our world. But we live in a time when evil is increasing instead of diminishing, when some men seem to be controlled by selfishness, madness, or evil forces. When the enemies of decent mankind are bent on subjugation of other men and women, righteous men and women must stand against evil. Please remember that the yoke of oppression is not lifted by prayer alone. God is our shepherd and we are his sheep. As long as there are wolves about, God will use some of us as sheep dogs to defend the rest of us. These stories are about people like that and the forces they fight against. The stories describe violence because it occurs in the real world and it is active in the lives of all people whether they recognize it or not.

To my non-Christian readers –

The Crossfire series include depictions of spiritual warfare and spiritual activity with which the non-Christian may not be familiar. These stories describe the realms and activities of both God and Satan because they are real and active in the lives of all people whether they recognize it or not.

Steve Thompson

CHAPTER ONE

The assault was timed to be unexpected. It happened in broad daylight rather than under the cover of darkness. The planners of the attack had done their homework and prepared for the NovaStar home defense system by cutting the power and phone lines to the house and blanketing the area with a radio-frequency scrambler signal to prevent calls for help by cell phone or radio signal. The raiders wore body armor complete with helmets and gauntlets to deter Tazer darts and had self-contained oxygen masks to avoid knockout gas.

Laura Malone had just completed a load of laundry and was making out checks for the monthly bills when the strident, two-tone alarm chimed telling her that intruders had come to call. She used the remote control to turn on the 60-inch television in the den and selected the NovaStar channel.

Laura was an elegant looking young woman with a full figure which she kept under control through exercise and diet. She was wearing blue jeans with a white sweater that set off her medium-length blonde hair. Her jade-green eyes which usually seemed to be full of humor were cold with fury this morning as she watched the men attacking her house. Leaning back in her chair she stretched her six foot tall frame as she punched in the combination on the gun safe in the wall of the den behind her. Taking out a dull-black, .45 caliber automatic, she jacked a shell into the chamber in a manner that showed her familiarity with this particular weapon. She had the fleeting thought that she had become so very familiar with a variety of killing weapons in the last year or so.

The twelve men attacking the house came in four separate teams. These were shown in four split screens with a fifth screen displaying alarms and responses. The cut power and phone lines were indicated in yellow as simply indications of actions. The actual power and phone lines to the house were buried far underground in armored conduits that were monitored by the system constantly for tampering. The radio frequency jamming

1

was also indicated but in yellow since the radio frequency communications for the house were handled by a line-of-sight satellite uplink rather than broadcast radio.

The attacker's dilemma was becoming quickly apparent to them as they weren't able to gain access to the house from any of the four directions. The view systems that let the people inside, see the world outside, didn't provide any windows for entry and the four doors were far more solid than any normal private home would have. Twelve inches of solid armor plate covered by a decorative wood appliqué were set into equivalent frames. Also, unknown to the raiders was the fact that if the outer door was attacked physically, a second portal guard slid into position behind the first. The second guard was twice as thick as and more unmovable than the first. As all four doors were presently suffering from battering, the second portal guards had already activated.

In the event that the attackers used explosives or rocket-propelled grenades, the facade of the outer walls hid the equivalent of an Abram's M2 Adiabatic tank armor at all points and under the full roof. They simply weren't going to get in.

Keying in Jack's code on the satellite communicator, Laura left him a short message. She knew he was working out at the dojo and his cell phone would be with his clothes in the locker room rather than on his person.

She then called 9-1-1 and warned the police to bring the SWAT team because these guys were well armed.

When the team at the side door brought out a cutting torch to work on the door she decided to teach them a lesson. She could see the body armor and the face shields and masks so she didn't waste time with the normal, low-level responses. She opted for a more effective greeting. She electrified the outer door with 50,000 volts at 10 amps. As the torch was applied to the door, the voltage travelled through the flame and gas to the fuel tank which promptly exploded. It wasn't too big a tank, so the damage was not lethal to the four men. After the video flare settled down, she could see two men sprawled on the ground not moving. The other two were staggering around holding various damaged parts. The force of the explosion was such that the fragments of the tank had impacted their body armor at such high speed it was like a sledge hammer. The fragments didn't penetrate the armor but the concussion from each piece was very harsh indeed.

She felt a jolt and looked at screen two which showed the back of the house. The team there had used some plastic explosives. The alarm level on the television screen was still in the yellow which meant they hadn't breached the outer door. She saw them scratching their heads at the lack of damage to the door. One of them was talking into a cell phone.

The lady 9-1-1 operator told her that units were now on the scene. Laura watched as the SWAT teams surrounded and apprehended ten of the men and examined and then handcuffed the two on the ground. She deactivated the second portals and went to meet the head of the SWAT team at the front door.

The Commander was examining the door when it opened and Laura stood there and smiled at him. He stood up and took his helmet off. "I've seen some sturdy doors in my time but this is a real work of art."

Laura replied, "That's the price one has to pay for peace of mind these days." She didn't want to tell him that over twelve million dollars of the eighteen million dollar price of the house was in the armor plating and defense systems. "Thank you for risking your neck arresting these people. Do you think they'll tell you why they were attacking my house? They seemed way too professional and coordinated to be break-in artists."

The Commander said that they would see what they could get out of the attackers at the station. But, he would need to have her fill out a report detailing what she knew about the attack.

Laura handed him a CD. "Everything I know is on that disc."

The Commander looked at the label and saw the NovaStar design. "Okay, if you'll just sign here, and here, and here, I'll be on my way."

The NovaStar Home Defense Systems were one of her husband's products that he had created in his "Technology Alternatives" plant in Littleton. The system had such successes that the demand was outpacing the supply. The NovaStar system wasn't a run-of-the-mill alarm system. It was a fully-legal home defense system that fought back against intruders and captured them. The police were more than impressed with the results and the fact that it video-tracked everything that happened during a break-in attempt.

The system even was able to provide coverage of the approach of the intruders prior to them setting off the system defenses. The CD would give both the police and the prosecuting attorney enough to convict the assailants.

Laura signed where indicated and waved good-bye to the police. She then reactivated the alarm system for the front door and headed for the garage. They hadn't bothered with the garage or the vehicles or the NovaStar system would have noted it. She took the newly acquired Cadillac SUV with its own armor plating and defensive systems and headed for the dojo in southeast Denver.

CHAPTER TWO

Jack Malone was sweating lightly. At 195 pounds, his six-foot, four-inch frame filled out the traditional martial arts outfit called a Gi. His adventures in the last year had added considerable muscle to both his arms and chest which buffed out his physique. His blonde hair was normally combed neatly back and made an excellent frame for his lean face which was dominated by intense gray-green eyes. Right now his hair was anything but combed or neat.

Jack had the dojo to himself this morning. Sensei Grady was in the Orient this month, studying new techniques. The other students and black belt teachers avoided Monday mornings for all the usual reasons.

His practice in various Katas had gone well and he was relaxed and confident as he completed the last one. After his morning run and exercise session he had come down here to practice. Honing his skills in the various martial arts, to the best level he could by himself, had always been important to him. He had to admit that he had learned that the translation of martial arts from the dojo to actual combat was a big jump. The real conflicts were much more intense being that they were usually life or death matters. He had more than his share recently.

A sound intruded on his senses and he stopped to determine what it was. In the quiet dojo he quickly identified the tiny sound as his cell phone in the locker room. He jogged over to the lockers and picked up the phone. Noting that the call was from home, he listened to the terse message. He wasn't too worried because she couldn't be in a safer place. But all the same, he wanted to be there with her so he threw on his street clothes.

Out of hard-learned caution he checked the streets outside from the window before leaving the building. He noticed two, almost identical, brown vans parked across the street from the dojo that had not there when he came in. Nothing unusual about the vans but, something was still tugging at his spirit. He was doubly cautious due to the attack on the house. He opened the front door to the dojo and started to step out. A slight blur of motion at the extreme limits of his peripheral vision made him step back into the dojo rather than out onto the front step. As he stepped back, two stun darts embedded themselves in the door frame, one on either side. Slamming the door and locking it, Jack took off for the rear entrance. Seeing movement out there he decided to use a little-known exit onto the second level roof instead of a door. Quickly running upstairs and to the back of the dojo, he looked out and couldn't detect anyone. Sliding out on the roof he peered over the edge of the roof and saw two men with stun guns pointed at the rear door. One of the men saw him on the roof and triggered a snap shot with his weapon. The dart sailed by Jack as he ducked back and imbedded itself in the roof of the house next door after completing its parabolic arc back towards the earth.

Grateful that at least they were trying to take him alive, Jack jumped up and ran around the roof to the front and jumped to the ground when he saw no one around the front of the building. He was about to head for his car when several men came around the side of the dojo and headed for him.

Two of them fired more darts at him. He stepped out of the path of the first one and caught the second on with the sleeve of his jacket. Now the other three men were upon him and they weren't being as gentle. They had clubs and sprayers of mace. Jack side-stepped the first club swing and used a Jujitsu technique to spin the man around while taking his club away. That unfortunate person managed to get sprayed with mace, and darted by his friends. To add insult to injury Jack then smacked him on the head with the borrowed club.

Moving constantly and quickly Jack hit the gunman trying to shoot darts. Jack's club struck the thug's arm with enough force to cause him to drop the gun. Then Jack hit him on the head hard enough to cause him to join his gun on the ground. The remaining attacker whirled a capture net at Jack to wrap him up. Jack did a low forward roll which avoided the net and at the same time allowed Jack to smash the man's foot with the club. The second stroke of the club was upward and shattered some of the man's teeth and laid the attacker out flat on his back.

There were two other men with dart guns running towards him which caused Jack to run into the alley behind the dojo to avoid their darts. As he ran past the back door of the dojo he saw that there was a large van completely blocking the alley twenty feet in front of him. He slid to a halt and turned around. The other two men ran into the alley behind him but suddenly turned around and ran the other direction for some reason. Then Jack saw an extremely large man coming up a set of stairs from a basement into the alley. The only problem with that is that there weren't any stairs there.

The man that had appeared was at least seven feet in height but also at least four feet in width. He looked like a larger version of the Hulk cartoon character except that this one wasn't green but black and he wasn't there for fun. He had a baleful look on his face and amused anger in his eyes.

He might have been a demon, a being from the spirit world, but he was something more than that because he was definitely interacting in the natural, physical world, unlike most beings from that dimension. The way the soda can he stepped on flattened out meant that he probably weighed over five hundred pounds and none of it was fat. His voice was a deep rumble. "Don't make me hurt you. Come along quietly." Total confidence in his ability to crush Jack was evident in his slow, casual approach which boxed Jack in between himself and the van.

Jack said, "I bind you in the name of the Lord Yahshua." The words didn't seem to have any effect on the huge man. He just frowned more and raised his huge arms to gather Jack in.

Just then a sweet, not-too-gentle, voice coming from behind the large man's back, said, "HEYYYY, pit-dweller, why don't you pick on somebody your own size?"

The large man spun around with an agility that was surprising for his bulk. He looked at the lovely woman standing in front of him with amusement.

Jack looked for points to attack the man from the back and honestly couldn't find anywhere he could do anything. The man's legs were so large and solid Jack doubted that he could break the guy's knee if he kicked him as hard as he could. But, Jack knew that woman's voice. He wasn't about to let this creature attack his wife without trying to do something.

Laura stood there in her white top and blue jeans with a hand on her left hip. Studying the man she added a second comment, "You had better go home while you can, Ugly. I'm sure they're missing you at the dung-heap."

Now, that irritated the large man and he started for this impudent girl with destruction in his heart. As he took the second step Jack saw a bright golden glow surround the man's bulk.

Laura started praying silently the Lord's Prayer and her armor flared into being. The sword appeared in her right hand and the glory of Yahveh was streaming from it in waves of white light. She started to advance on the creature which had stopped walking and started back peddling quickly. Not wanting to get crushed by accident, Jack saw an opening and dropped to the ground and rolled under the van.

The dark man seemed to shrink in the bright white light exploding from the sword and he turned to his right and dived towards where the ground and building met. But he seemed to melt into both and disappeared from sight.

Jack came out from under the truck as Laura's armor faded from view and the sword disappeared. She came over and hugged him. He said, "Thanks, I don't think I could have taken him." He looked at the somber expression on Laura's face and noticed a residual golden hue to her eyes. "I think we need to talk."

As they walked out of the alley he noticed the two dart gun men that had made haste to leave when the big guy showed up, laying on the ground unconscious. He looked at Laura. She smiled, "Best exercise I've had for a month." Noting the worried look on his face she shrugged, "You taught me well. They didn't stand a chance."

Jack didn't even bother calling the police since the alley incident would be extremely hard to describe and even harder to prove. They each got into their vehicles and drove carefully, very carefully back to their house in the suburbs.

CHAPTER THREE

Sarah Connelly was what the young men today would call a "hottie". She stood five-foot, ten-inches tall with a well-defined figure and legs of a dancer. Her face was classically beautiful with full lips and a solid jaw. Lustrous black hair, cut in a short style, framed her face and slender neck. Her brown eyes showed an intelligence that made many men decide not to confront her. Her attitude was slightly aggressive, bordering on pushy. But, as a former Mossad agent she could carry that attitude with assurance. Normally her mind was extremely focused.

At this moment she was in a definitely detached frame of mind. She knew what was happening but felt as if she were completely separate from the event. In a way, the detachment ruled out any fear, but at the same time, in her mind, it indicated a terrible lack of focus.

Her car was upside down and smashed beyond recognition. She had been spared major injury, in great part, due to the design of the new armored Cadillac SUV and the safety restraints and air bags. But, now that the vehicle had come to rest, her problem was the men trying to get to her from outside the car. They weren't interested in helping her, they were trying to kill her by any means they could.

It was their vehicle that had crashed into hers at seventy miles an hour. She had momentarily glanced at a map. Seeing their chance they immediately swerved towards her SUV. They were professionals. She had not had a clue that they were setting her up. It was a classic two-car smash and grab. She could have kicked herself because she hadn't noticed their rapid approach from two lanes away. They smashed into her right front fender.

The power and weight of the pickup they were driving was sufficient to overcome her counter steering and shoved her to the left. That's when the small sports car on her left and directly in front of her car slammed on its brakes. Her left front tire climbed the back end of the smaller car which sent the Cadillac airborne and rolling to its right. She fought the centripetal force and slapped the EWANS button on the dash as the car flew upward. The emergency warning and notification system sent an emergency signal to a base receiver in a burst transmission. She knew the car had to be upright for the signal to reach the satellite but then she figured it probably was upright a couple of times, briefly, as it spiraled through the air.

After it hit the ground, the first two rolls weren't too bad as all the glass exploded outward away from her and the body deformed. But then the pickup smashed into her upside down SUV and propelled it off the road into a large ditch, full of car-sized boulders. Caroming off the first rock, drove the front end directly into the next one, and the Cadillac instantly compacted to two-thirds its normal length and came to a halt upside down with the roof crushed down to the door sills.

This was now a problem for the attackers. They couldn't be sure she was dead and they couldn't get the doors open on either side because they were jammed shut, both vertically and lengthwise, by the crash and the car was jammed between two major boulders.

After trying unsuccessfully to open the doors, they tried to shoot through the armor-plated doors without success. Now they were trying to puncture the gas tank and set the car on fire to finish the job for sure.

Sarah was out of her seat belt but upside down and closely confined to the front seat area. The roof was crushed up to the top of the upside down seat backs and dash. Blood from a cut on her neck kept dripping into her eyes which interfered with her thinking. She thought "Why can't I get cut on the back of my head, then it wouldn't bother me so much!" She knew that there was armor plating on the bottom of the vehicle as a protection against mines. The armored bottom kept them from shooting through the bottom but it also kept her from getting out that way. She realized she was in an armor-plated coffin with no way out. That was the reason for the detachment of her mind.

She could hear them talking outside. "She's probably dead! Nobody could have lived through that, anyway."

The second voice was insistent. "We have our orders. We got to see the body or we will become bodies, get it?"

First voice continued to complain. "How are we going to see in there? The thing is armor plated and pretty much welded together. We don't have the gear to get it open. Anyway, we ain't heard a sound out of her. I tell you she's deader than a rock in there!"

The other voice started to answer. "Look, you know the orders... Oh crap, it's the cops."

A new voice joined in, "Is there somebody in that car?"

Second voice answered back. "We don't know. It's crushed pretty badly and we can't get it open."

The policeman told them. "Okay, you've done what you could. Come up here and give me a statement about what you saw."

The voices faded away and Sarah kept working her left arm around her hip until she could get to the cell phone in her pocket. She then had to find room to move it down to her face to see if it was still working. It was! She dialed 9-1-1 and waited. Getting the 9-1-1 operator, she explained where she was and that the men the police officer was talking to were the ones that caused the accident and that they were armed and had been shooting at her car in the ditch.

A minute later she heard the loudspeaker on the police car emit a double note tone. She waited expectantly and was rewarded by a call for the men to raise their hands and to put their weapons down. This call was answered by gunfire. But from the number of shots and the different calibers she could identify, it sounded like the police were holding their own in the battle.

Several minutes later the 9-1-1 operator told her that the police had the suspects under arrest and that a tow truck would be there any minute.

Actually it took more than forty-five minutes before the tow truck got the smashed SUV out of the rocks in the ditch and turned right-side up onto the three wheels it still possessed. By then the fire department was there but having a real problem with the Jaws of Life. They just couldn't quite separate the body panels or the doors or the top. They changed tactics and soon she could smell the aroma of burned paint and hot metal as they torched off the driver's door from its hinges.

They finally separated the door from the car and one of the EMTs half crawled in to see if she was too damaged to move. She surprised him by wiggling out between him and the seat. This caused her dress to climb all the way up to her head and she was sure the onlookers got a real good look at her underwear, but she wasn't going to stay in there one second more than necessary. Climbing to her feet she felt dizzy and grabbed onto the EMT as he stood up. He grabbed her around the waist and helped her over to the rescue squad.

After a few minutes she felt better and eyeballing the people around her, she declined a trip to the hospital for a checkup. She convinced them she was fine when the second EMT, a tall woman, grasped her right arm to help her get into the door of the rescue truck. In one smooth move Sarah broke free of the hold, grabbed the EMT's arm, and cranked it up behind the EMT's back. She leaned forward and quietly spoke into the woman's ear. "I said, no. Now take a hint before you are the one needing service, understand?" The woman nodded her head and Sarah released her arm.

Staying close to the police and the other emergency vehicles, she called Mark. He answered on the first ring. "Sarah, are you all right?"

She sighed, "Yes, I'm all right, but we're going to have to ask the CIA for new car."

He was quiet a second, "I just got the EWANS alert and am headed to your location now. I should be there in less than four minutes."

She told him where she was in the crowd and hung up.

The ranking police officer, a Captain, corralled her then and was insistent on her accompanying him to the state police office to explain why these men would attack her and then fire on his officers. "Mrs. Connelly, I'm afraid that I must insist on your going with me. And I wouldn't suggest you try any of those martial arts tricks on me like you did the med tech."

He radiated confidence and authority and was not going to let this woman talk him out doing things his way.

Sarah smiled at him and said that she would be glad to meet him there later, after she tied up some loose ends."

He shook his head. Whatever else he was going to say was lost in the roar of helicopter rotors as a fully-armed MH-53J Pavelow III combat helicopter landed on the road within twenty feet of the police cars. A fully armed Apache helicopter hovered thirty feet above the road with its weapons trained on the assembly by the wrecked Cadillac.

The Captain lost some of his composure when he saw that these weren't conventional EMS or police helicopters but fully-armed military war birds. It didn't help his perspective when the right hand doors of the first chopper opened and Mark and two Special Forces types jumped out and jogged over to them. Like the other two, Mark was in full combat gear and had an M4 assault rifle with a 40mm grenade launcher in his hands. It was obvious that Mark was all military and deadly serious. The helmet he had on was a combat flight helmet with the visor down. As he approached the group he slid the dark visor up and locked it. The other two men spread out and stood watching everyone else. As a sensible precaution, the police in the area kept their hands away from their side arms.

Walking up to Sarah, Mark asked her if she was all right. After she nodded she indicated the State Police Captain and said, "This officer is on the verge of arresting me to make sure I go with him."

All at once a four-wheel-drive SUV climbed over the divider in the highway from the southbound lanes and headed directly for the crowd. Seeing it, the prisoners broke loose from the police officers holding them and ran for the SUV. From the back of the SUV a sub-machine gun started firing toward the crowd near Sarah, to keep the police from recapturing the prisoners.

Mark's head snapped to the left as the SUV headed towards them. He spoke into the combat microphone at the corner of his mouth. "Eagle two, take them out, NOW!"

The Apache had already noticed the SUV and had rotated where it was. It fired a single missile from the racks under its landing rails. The missile crossed the distance in less than a second and impacted on the windshield of the on-rushing Ford Explorer. Even though the SUV had been accelerating towards them, the missile explosion knocked the vehicle backwards and instantly gutted the machine. All the glass blew outward along with pieces of the interior as the roof exploded straight up into the air. A shattered ball of fire, the destroyed vehicle bounced back into the median and came to a rest, sending black smoke upward in a dense cloud.

Mark handed Sarah his rifle and turned back to the Police Captain. It didn't make the policeman feel any better, when Sarah showed she knew how to handle the weapon as she moved it into the port arms position very naturally, with her finger resting just outside the trigger and her thumb on the fire selector switch.

Mark read the officer's name tag. "Captain Alworth, I am General Mark Connelly of the U.S. Air Force. My wife is in much more danger than you can understand, presently. I am taking her with me. You have my word that we will be at your office later today to go over the situation. But, as you can see, the people that attacked her are sufficiently crazy to strafe or blow up everyone here, including you, to get to her. For everyone's protection she needs to go with me, for now."

Mark stared at the man, "If you want, I can go through the chain of command and have your superiors tell you the same thing but it would waste a lot of valuable time during which there will be an unacceptable exposure for all of us."

The officer looked from his face to her holding the rifle and thought about the situation. He noted the military designations on the aircraft and knew they were combat designations which he recognized from his time in the Marines. Legally, he was fairly sure he had the right to tell the General no, but he was smart enough to know he couldn't back up his authority. "Okay, General, I have your word she will come in today?"

Mark nodded and turned to Sarah. He took the rifle back and he and the other two men provided cover for her as they left. In the midst of the weapons and the matte black and military camouflage green, she looked like an innocent vision in her rumpled pale pink business suit. She walked to the helicopter with her head held high. The three men walked backward, watching the gathering crowd for signs of trouble. They reached the armored airship and got onboard. The chopper lifted quickly, straight up, side-slipped to the right and gathered airspeed as it moved away from the scene.

As Captain Alworth watched the helicopters disappear over the trees, his second in command moved over near him and said, "You really know how to pick the beauties, don't you?" Alworth shook his head, "Tell me about it." He was just glad he was alive and still had his job. "Get some more troopers out here. I want to find out who is nuts enough to attack us while there were two Combat helicopters standing guard. And while you're at it, find out what you can about that General Connelly and his wife. She must be important to have connections like that. But, I'll bet you dollars to doughnuts that it will be federally protected information."

He turned and started organizing the collection of cars, fire trucks, wrecks, prisoners, and crowd control. Glancing at the fiercely burning SUV in the median, he was sure he didn't have to worry about the shooters that had been in it.

On the helicopter Mark took his helmet off and held Sarah's face in his hands and tenderly kissed her. "Lady Spy, you scared the life right out of me with that EWANS signal. I realized right then that in my life you are the most important thing in this world!" He hugged her again and she felt his conviction that he had been really worried about her. That conviction made her feel secure and loved. It also hurt where she had been bruised. Overall though, she was very pleased that he was glad to see her alive and well.

She held his hands and took one and kissed it. "I'm sorry. I wasn't too pleased with the situation myself. Did you see the Cadillac?"

He nodded and turned and poked Major Mike, White who was piloting the helicopter, in the ribs. "See, I told you that was a good truck. It looked like two giants had played basketball with it but she was safe." He turned back to his wife, "We have got to get another one of those for you."

Sarah smiled and looked at the two other military personnel behind them. She nodded slightly and smiled at them both. Both men still had their visors down and were scanning the air and land around the chopper for threats or missile launches. Each one gave her a small salute to say 'you're welcome' and went back to the serious business at hand. She relaxed and leaned back in the seat. She felt sore and could feel the bruises and bumps starting to let her know that she had been in an accident. But what she felt most was anger. This attack was not going to go unpunished!

That afternoon they made their promised trip to the state police headquarters and Officer Alworth. It was mostly paperwork because she really couldn't shed any light on whom the attackers were or why they wanted her dead. Officer Alworth confirmed that they were waiting to interrogate the attackers after they were out of the hospital, but the four men weren't cooperating and already had attorneys present, which made it difficult to get any serious information from them. They were complaining that the whole thing was simply an accident and they were trying to help her. They fired back at the police because they thought the policemen weren't really police. They had concealed weapons permits, but the whole thing was obviously a load of horse manure.

One interesting note was that all four of the attackers, the two in the hospital, the one in jail, and the one in the morgue, each had a drawing on them. Officer Alworth opened an evidence envelope and pulled two of the drawings out. They were Xeroxes of a hand drawn picture. Mark looked at the subject of the drawing and then at Sarah. The drawing clearly depicted a small, long wooden box. The box was open with a clasp on the front, and inside was a large nail or spike. They shrugged their shoulders and the drawings went back into the envelope.

An hour later they called Jack and Laura Malone. Upon hearing about the attacks on them at the same time as the one on Sarah, they drove down to the Malones for a conference.

After they each told their stories, they batted the problem around. Since this seemed to be a concerted attack to get the nail from them it was based in the spiritual more than the secular world. Jack said, "I still don't understand what is so important about the crucifixion nail that people would kill to get it."

Laura reminded him of what the demonic power behind the Omniscience Temple had said to her when he had captured her on Baffin Island. *"You really don't have a clue as to the importance of that piece of metal, do you?"*

The four of them decided to stay there that night as it was the safest place they knew. They would pray for protection and go see the Minister the next morning. Jack called and made an appointment with Minister Throman for 10 a.m.

CHAPTER FOUR

The 78-year old Christian Minister, Alan Throman, listened to the accounts of the attacks and then their questions as to the actual importance of the crucifixion nail. In prayer, he asked the Holy Spirit for guidance and revelation knowledge concerning the present day meaning of the metal spike that had once helped to pin the body of Christ to the cross.

The Minister looked to be about sixty, but his real age was closer to eighty. His wispy white hair framed a peaceful face that had seen its share of hardships and spiritual combat. His congregation knew him as a fellow Christian who made an effort to help everyone have a deep, intimate relationship with the Lord Jesus. He didn't offer to be a "high priest" for them and intercede for them with Yahveh. He told them plainly. "You and you alone hold your life and accountability to the Lord. You need to know Him now. Later it will be too late. Our "high priest" is the Lord Jesus Christ."

After considering what he discerned and what it meant, he thanked the Lord for the knowledge and sighed. Looking at the four younger Christians, he explained the insight he had gotten. "All that I can give you for sure is really not much more than a direction in which to continue your search."

The Minister steepled his fingers and continued, "In the spiritual world, the nail is a connector to the crucifixion event. I believe that could mean it can allow a spirit, an angel or a demon, to have access to something that occurred at that time. Remember that the passage of time was created by Yahveh for the people of this universe, not for the spirit world. There is a relationship between our time and their activities because we are the focus of spiritual activity and we move in time even if they don't."

He got up from his desk and paced back and forth, to keep his body busy, while he tried to think the concept through on the mental plane. "In today's world, some two thousand years after the fact, there aren't many things that are directly related to the spilling of Christ's blood, the cross, or the resurrection. We have the Bible, tons of hearsay, implied facts, reported events, and even scientifically authenticated histories of the crucifixion of the Lord. But this "treasure" is the only thing I am aware of that was physically there and is physically here, now. I think that there is something in each of our spirits that wants to touch greatness. That's why people all over the world pay great sums of money to acquire antiquities and other relics. They couldn't tell you about it, but I believe somewhere down inside of them, they feel the "connector" dimension of the item and want to be a part of that connection."

He looked to see if they understood what he was getting at. It appeared they did. "Okay, since it is a physical object that has spanned the centuries, from then to now, it is a physical connection. I don't pretend to understand how things work in the spirit world so I can't be too helpful at this point, but it seems reasonable to say that if the nail was there, and lasted till now in the physical realm, whatever spiritual importance it accrued by being part of the event, has lasted until now and possibly grown in importance in the spiritual realm, as its uniqueness became more unique. What that importance could be, may not be something we will understand before we meet Christ."

Jack, listening to the minister, attempted to summarize his concept. "What you mean is that we humans may not have the capacity to understand what is so important about this nail in the spiritual world, but that we should govern our actions concerning it as if it has a verifiable value, which is obviously very great in that kingdom, gauged by the unrelenting efforts of the enemy to acquire it. Is that about it?"

Alan nodded, "Right, considering the warfare and resources attributed to getting their hands on it, they think it has some supreme importance."

Jack continued to think it through. "There is also the possibility that the Lord prefers that we don't know what the importance is for reasons we can't understand but are for our own best interests."

Alan slapped his hands together. "Yes, you are beginning to see the limitations of ours that He has to work with, at the same time the faith to know that he works for our good outside of our understanding."

Mark commented, "I for one am very glad I'm not Yahveh. I wouldn't have the patience to work with us for very long."

Laura laughed, "That is why He's Yahveh and we're not. But, I agree with you Mark, I am so glad He carries the burden rather than me, for almost everything I do."

Sarah had been quietly praying and listening at the same time. Another holdover trait from her Mossad days was being good at doing one thing while thinking deeply about another. "I think part of the importance of the nail has to do with the direct physical contact it had with the Lord's body and blood. If there is a spiritual "imprint" of those things contained in the physical substance of the nail, then there would be some form of access for a spiritual force to use that imprint, either then or now."

Mark frowned, "The past is fixed, how could there be any effect back then, by any connection from now?"

Jack shook his head. "We don't know that the past is fixed. It only seems that way. Consider this; if time travel were real and I went back in time and prevented my grandparents from ever meeting, I create a single timeline paradox. How could I have been born to go back and stop them, if they hadn't met and created my mother or father? One theory is multiple timelines, where in timeline one, I am born and go back to interfere with my grandparents. Timeline two is created when I change things and create a world where one of my parents, and therefore I myself, never exist. To the people of timeline two, it seems fixed that my grandparents never met, created my ancestor, or me. I don't know that something like that could happen in the spiritual world considering that time isn't one of their dimensions."

Laura smiled at her husband, "I'm not sure I follow all of that but are you implying that Satan could possibly attempt to change things during the crucifixion if he gets this imprint or nexus that is part of the nail?"

Jack answered, "Possibly. "If he did change things, then we might never know that something was changed.

To us, the change would be the correct history. I doubt that Yahveh is going to allow him to do anything like that, though."

Alan stared at the floor and sighed. "Possibly, and just as possibly, Yahveh is counting on us to see that the enemy never gets the chance to do something like that." He looked up at them. "Has it occurred to you that He is counting on you to keep it safe?"

Mark, ever the practical thinker, said, "Why don't we just destroy it, melt it down so that Satan never gets the chance to use it?"

Alan shook his head, "What if its continued existence is beneficial in ways we don't understand? If we destroy it without Yahveh's leading, then we may sin a great sin. He has kept it safeguarded throughout the centuries and has put it in your hands because He wants it to be there. If He wanted it destroyed, it would never have gotten to us. He just may be counting on us to defend this nexus, or portal, or whatever it is."

Jack sighed, "I think you are right Alan. It rings true in my spirit and I have a peace about knowing that it is important. I don't care why it is important, because I trust Yahveh and He thinks it's important. That is enough for me."

Mark stood up and walked over to Jack; he got down on one knee and put his hand on Jack's, on the arm of the chair. "I'm not sure I understand this "connector" theory but I can tell you this. My spirit agrees with your last statement and I pledge my loyalty and my life to helping you protect Yahveh's Holy Treasure." The other three joined in and agreed that they too would do their best, individually or together, to see that the nail never came into the possession of the evil one.

Jack nodded, "It is agreed then." Thinking for a second he grinned and said, "I feel like Frodo in the "Fellowship of the Ring" when the eight others agreed to accompany him to Mordor. Oh great! That, of course, makes me the ring bearer".

Alan smiled, "You don't know how accurate that similarity could be." His spirit was troubled by the winds of spiritual power loosened by the advance of the enemy, in the quest to gain the nail.

He looked at each of them. "Remember, these are the last of the last days and evil is growing in the land. This is as the Bible prophesies: *"But know this that in the last days, perilous times will come"*. Read James 3:1-9 to see what I'm talking about."

Jack brought up the encounter with the being in the alley. "I don't understand two things. How could it come out of the ground and go back into it like a spirit, yet be a solid being affecting our world. Also, I don't know why the name of the Lord didn't affect it."

Alan nodded, "Well, again I'm not sure but I will look into that more. You recall that the Lord's body was able to pass through locked doors, yet was physical enough to touch and for him to eat. I'm guessing that this man/creature you encountered had a body similar to that, but, from the dark side. He obviously could have hurt you and at the same time, Laura's armor and sword frightened him enough he fled, very curious."

The team decided to return to "Castle Malone", as Mark was calling it, and determine what the best course should be in light of the attacks and their new determination to protect the treasure.

CHAPTER FIVE

After a light dinner they discussed everything that had occurred and brain-stormed ideas on how to find out who was behind the attacks.

Mark suggested, "What if we track the attackers after they get bailed out? I think I can get the type of gear we need for that type of surveillance."

Jack agreed with that thought. "We can't get at them in jail and with their lawyers they'll be out soon enough." He picked up the phone and checked his palm pilot for the number to Captain Alworth. After punching in the number, he got the policeman on the second ring. "Captain Alworth? I'm an aide to General Connelly and he was wondering when the court dates will be set for the people who attacked his wife and if they are going to be released on bail." He listened for a few minutes and he ended the call.

He smiled at Mark, "You'd better get your gear quickly, because those guys are getting out on bail at six p.m. tonight."

While they were preparing to track the enemy agents the phone rang. Jack answered it and heard the voice of his dad. "Jack, how are things going?"

"Like normal dad, we all were attacked by an enemy and Sarah was almost killed in a car wreck they arranged. We're about to see if we can find out who is behind these attacks."

His dad paused to think about all that. "Wow, sounds like you have your plate full right now. Is there anything we can do?"

"Right now, just pray for protection and success. You might think about the fact that you and Uncle Larry were involved with the Holy Treasure, too. They might try to take you for leverage or whack you for revenge."

Steve Malone considered that. "Okay, we'll take some precautions on that front. Look, I called for a different reason. You remember the agreement I made with the Lord about building a church in the mountains, there in Colorado?"

Jack thought about that. "Yeah, you said something like, if the Lord gave you ten or twenty million dollars, you would build Him a church in the mountains here. But didn't you have some pretty bizarre plans for that?"

After a slight pause, Jack's dad responded with, "Bizarre". "No, I like to think of them as progressive rather than quirky. Anyway, thanks to the sales of the NovaStar systems, I have gone well over the fourteen million dedicated to this project and feel compelled to get started on it. I would like to work with you on the design and location of the building as well as the logistics. It would have some of the elements of your "Lord's Lunchbox."

Jack smiled at the reference to the open eating area he had established in downtown Denver for the homeless. It was totally automatic, with no people present, except for a protector that seemed to be like a guardian angel, who only showed up when needed. "Well, actually dad, I gave some thought to that concept several years ago and will send you my notes. But right now is not a good time for us. I'll call you when we get a break on this thing. Will that be all right?"

"Sure, I understand. Don't worry about it for the next couple of weeks, anyway, since I have to research a property and acquire it before we can start planning the building. I'll call you when we get that established. Tell your lovely wife hello, and also your friends, the Connelly's."

"Okay dad, just be careful. These guys tried to take me alive but they tried to kill Sarah and they might do either to you guys. If you run into trouble along these lines, call me right then, all right? I love you Dad and I've put everyone in the family in harm's way by this burden. I don't want you hurt."

"I love you, too, Son. Just remember that you didn't pick this burden up until Yahveh gave it to you. You have no guilt in bringing these troubles to us. This is all part of Yahveh's plan and we should praise Him for it. He used it to bring you to Him, remember?"

Jack smiled at the memory and they finished the phone call. Laura looked at him as she got the food packed into a backpack and tipped her head to one side in the obvious question. He smiled, "That was Dad. He wants to get started on a project here in Colorado and wants my help in getting it going. I told him we were a little busy right now but we'll see in a couple of weeks. He's going to look for land to purchase during that time, anyway. He said to tell you "Hello" and that he sends his love." Jack turned to Mark and Sarah who were ready and waiting to leave. "He also said to tell you guys hello too. He is glad that Sarah came through the attack without any injuries and asks you both to be careful and walk in the anointing and protection of Yahshua."

They agreed with Jack's dad. They were ready to pick up the tracking gear that Mark had arranged for, while they got ready to go. But, Steve Malone's comments reminded them to pray for success and protection before they started out. This prayer reminded them that they were refreshing their minds to the fact that the battle is the Lord's.

CHAPTER SIX

As the evening chill began to settle over the greater Denver area, one of the four men that attacked Sarah walked out of the Denver County Jail with his lawyer. Talking quietly to themselves, they walked quickly over to a Lincoln Town Car and got in. The driver was trained to spot any type of surveillance and to shake them off. He watched the other cars as they left the jail area and soon was well out of sight of anyone who might be trying to follow them. He took a circuitous route that gave him the opportunity to check his backtrack several times.

They were on the loose. Nobody had followed them. He informed the two men in the back seat, who, for whatever reason, looked behind them to apparently confirm the driver's opinion. Now sure they weren't being watched, the recent bailees gave the driver a specific address on the north side of downtown. The driver turned the big car in the right direction, still casually checking for a tail.

The team had no problem tailing the big car and had never lost sight of their quarry since he stepped out of the jail. The fact that they were in Major Mike's USAF helicopter had quite a bit to do with the fact that the driver never knew they were there. Not only was it quiet but it was also over two thousand feet above the car. The half mile altitude was not a problem to the gyro-stabilized, laser-locked video system that made it seem like they were right on top of the Lincoln.

Mark noted that the car was now heading north on I-25 through the downtown area. They apparently felt safe because they had stopped just wandering around on the side streets and were definitely going somewhere.

The Lincoln exited the Interstate at 70th Street and headed east. After a mile and a half, they turned into the parking lot of an eight-story business building. The man and his lawyer exited the car and went into the building while the driver parked the Lincoln to wait for them. It was now after seven p.m. and the majority of the people in the building had called it a day and left the area. Mike White flipped two switches, which changed the input to the video screen, from optics to FLIR thermal imaging. By dropping down in height but still staying far enough away to not be detected, the Major was able to track the two heat sources as they made their way to a suite of offices on the second floor in the back of the building.

Mark had Mike do a quick vertical drop into a nearby parking lot and let both him and Jack get out. The helicopter lifted right back into the darkening sky with very little rotor noise or engine noise. Still, they had scared the water out of two teenagers in a car directly in front of where the chopper came down. They had been making out when the heavily armed war bird settled down twenty feet in front of them with all guns and missiles pointed in their direction. Mark went over and told them that this operation was government business and to forget that they had seen anything. They agreed and quickly drove away from the pair of camouflaged men.

Jack and Mark hustled across the street and around the building between them and their target. Closing on the business building the two men had entered, they pushed their way into the lobby on their side of the structure. Jack looked at the directory and came up with at least three names on the second floor that could be the name of the suite where the men had gone into. Finding the stairs they jogged up to the second floor and eased out onto the balcony-like walk that circled the four story atrium.

Moving carefully, they were able to determine which suite the men had entered. The sign next to the door proclaimed that the business inside was Indispensable Industries Incorporated with a big number three embossed over a large san-serif letter "L". Seeing no one around, Mark walked quickly over to the doors and found them locked. Stepping back he took out a small, handheld version of the thermal imaging system, with which they had been watching their quarry from the helicopter.

Seeing three green blobs over to the far right of the office he walked down the balcony walkway until he was even with them. They were in an office that was next to the janitorial services room. This was also locked but gave way quickly to Mark's expertise. He and Jack entered the room and closed the door. Finding a light switch, Jack turned on the glaring fluorescent overhead lights. Mark used the scope again and walked around the cleaning equipment until he was as near as he could get to the people on the other side of the wall. Putting the scope away he pulled out a small amplifier equipped with an earphone. He pressed the input for the eavesdropper against the wall and was rewarded with a fairly clear rendition of the conversation going on in the next room. He plugged a second earphone into the amp and gave it to Jack so that they could both listen.

One of the men, obviously a boss-type, was doing most of the talking. "Look, I don't care if you're tired of telling me what happened. You're going to keep going over it until I'm satisfied. Understand?"

The second voice said something like, "Sure, sure, whatever. We were in place like you told us to be, right near the highway, when we see the broad go by in the big SUV you described. Her husband ain't with her, but we decide to whack her anyway, because that was the fallback plan. We set it up on the radio with Zero in the sports car, and when we see her looking at a map we drove into her car. It worked great and Zero hit his brakes causing the SUV to flip up into the air. The thing comes down and starts to roll, once, twice, and then I punched it and hit the cart-wheeling broad, broadside, if you know what I mean. The SUV is being flattened like a pancake but is not stopping. So, I tapped it and it went into some big rocks and smashed to a halt. That's when Sam and I got out and tried to make sure the broad was dead. But the thing is so smashed together we can't get into it to see. We tried shooting through the doors but they were bulletproof. It was the same with the bottom. We were just going to open the gas tank and set the whole thing on fire when the cop shows up. He pulls us away from the car and we're thinking we bettered get out of there before some bystander tells the cop that we did it. The cop gets a call on his car radio and before we can disappear, he draws down on us. Well, I don't want to answer questions, so I unload on the trooper, but he's got one of those bulletproof Mustangs and now two more cops show up and there's a short gunfight, with us getting the losing end. Wally got whacked and then Mace and Eddy went down. That's when I gave up before we were all dead and there wasn't anybody to tell you what happened."

The boss was quiet for a minute while he thought about the story. Then he decided, "Well, it looks like you made a total screw-up of the whole thing!"

The other man protested, "No way, we did everything you told us to do. How were we to know that the car would completely seal us out? How?

The other voice came right back, "Did you take explosives like I also told you to do?"

"Yeah, we did, but they were back in the truck and the cop showed up too quick to get them, let alone use them."

The boss chewed on that for a bit, then, "All right, we can't get into their house, and now they'll be watching for anything on the street. We need some leverage. Here's a list of other people that we can use to make the Malones see things our way. Now this time, quietly get these people and bring them here. No more screw-ups or you just ran out of reasons to be using up the air in the room." The voice turned cold. "Do we understand each other?"

"Yeah, we understand each other." There was the movement of chairs and other noises that indicated the meeting was over and people were getting ready to leave the office. Mark looked at Jack as he put the amplifier away. "I'm not going to let that weasel get out of here with that list."

Jack agreed. "I want to talk to that character that gave the orders, too." They made their way to the door and cracked it open. No one was out of the other office yet. They left the janitorial closet and quickly bracketed the other office doors just as they started to open.

Mark charged into the first two men leaving the office and smashed his pistol into the side of the lawyer's head. The man dropped like a puppet with the strings cut. The other man spun around and pulled a knife. Jack caught the third man as he tried to help the first two with Mark. Using a jujitsu technique, Jack spun the heavily set man around to his left and directly into a wall. The guy hit the wall hard enough to crack the paneling and fell straight backwards to the floor. Jack stuck his foot under the guy's head so that he didn't knock his brains out on the marble floor.

By this time Mark had closed on the second man and they fought silently, at first. The man was a formidable fighter. Mark blocked the knife thrust and knocked the knife from the man's hand. The character punched Mark in the gut with a hard left fist. Mark grunted but it didn't really hurt him. The man bounced back and took a fighter's stance. He motioned to Mark to come and fight him, "I don't know who the (deleted) you think you are friend, but you're dead meat!" Mark smiled a cold smile and holstered his pistol. "I'll bet that's what you and your friends told my wife, too."

The man peered harder in the dim lighting in the hall at Mark, and shrugged. "I'll take care of your widow for you right after they bury you." Mark stepped forward and the man swung a hard right round house punch for his head. Mark blocked the punch with his left arm and hit the man with a solid palm-heel strike to the chest. Mark had less than ten percent body fat and he weighed two hundred and fifteen pounds. Coupled with his fighting ability, which he had been honing since he entered the service a decade before, the punch carried a mean load. The other man flew off of his feet and into the railing of the walkway. He was on the way to the floor when he hit the railing with the back of his neck. There was a soft "crunch" and the man fell to the floor to his right and smashed his face into the tile flooring without putting a hand out to stop himself.

Mark walked over and checked the man's pulse. It was there and his eyes looked focused but he didn't move. Mark carefully checked the man's neck and whistled softly. The man had broken his neck and had lost the use of his body from the neck down. He hadn't lost the ability to breathe so he wasn't dead, but he just as well could have been. Mark checked the man's coat pocket and found the list he was carrying. The lawyer slept through the fight with a good sized knot on the side of his head.

Mark pulled both of the men into the office after Jack hauled the other one in, then Mark closed and locked the doors. Mark then secured the lawyer's hands and feet with plastic ties and gagged him. The fighter was rolling his eyes back and forth but apparently could no longer talk, either. Just to make sure, Mark secured him, too. Jack took the large man back to the office they had been in before and dumped the unconscious man on the floor.

Jack ripped the jacket and shirt off of the large man and they laid him on the conference room table. Mark took out his interrogation kit and injected the man in the arm.

Mark kept an eye on the man on the table while he walked over to Jack. He whispered, "We're getting into a rut here having to shoot guys up to find out what is going on. Why don't you go out in the other room and let Major White and the others know what we're doing?"

Jack agreed and went out of the room. Jack came back and told Mark quietly. "They understand and are standing by."

Mark looked up at Jack questioningly, "What about fuel? Are they going to have to refuel soon?"

Jack smiled, "No, Mike set it down on an empty Helio pad about two miles from here and talked the owner into refueling him for a few extra bucks."

Mark nodded, checked the sedated man, he was ready. They started questioning him.

Twenty minutes later they were back in the chopper and airborne over Denver.

CHAPTER SEVEN

Mark hugged Sarah and let Jack relate what they had done and found out from the truth serum session. He did whisper in her ear, "There's one that won't bother you, again."

Jack told them about their eavesdropping on the conversation and the brief skirmish on the walkway. Then he got to the interrogation.

"The man we interrogated was named Marco Delaiss. He is the middle man in a front company for a conglomeration of Muslim terrorists groups around the world. He was given a commission to find the crucifixion nail, and kill everyone associated with us in the process. The principle wants us," He indicated Laura and himself, "alive for their personal satisfaction in killing us."

Mark added, "They don't know about Stan and Debbie but they do know about Sensei Grady and Minister Throman." He pulled out the list he had taken from the paralyzed man. "They have Jack's father and his uncle on their hit list, as well as Carol Nolan and me. They don't mention Sarah, which is strange since they tried to kill her." He slapped the list against his leg. "You know what this is? This is a list of the people involved in the Don Miland operation!"

Jack nodded, "It doesn't seem to take into account the people we've been involved with or that have helped us since then so, I think you've right, this is somehow related to that time."

Sarah asked Mark, "But I thought you said that everyone involved, at least on the other side, were wiped out by the explosion?"

Laura shook her head. "Not everyone. John Dalman survived and was on the loose for several weeks before he was killed in Chicago. He could have named all those names to someone else before he died. Remember how he hated us?" Jack agreed with her, "I think she's right. He would be one to try for revenge, but I doubt that he knew about the nail. I think Jack kept that to himself pretty much, because of the demon living in his house. Of course, the demon survived and could be behind this."

Mark added, "Don't forget about Whitey, our Judas goat."

Major White waved for their attention. "Where do we go now?"

Mark thought about that. "Can you put us down somewhere so we can think this out or does daddy want the car home by midnight?"

Mike laughed, "No problem, this sweet little bucket and I are at your beck and call until the base commander changes his mind, General Connelly." Mike smiled at Mark's rank which the President had not decided to take back after promoting the entire team in their last effort.

Mark smiled. "Okay, find a nice private place where we won't be disturbed for a while."

Mike said, "Your wish is my command General". The chopper suddenly lost speed and descended quickly over downtown Denver. Adroitly landing the bird on a dark Helio port on top of one of the highest buildings in downtown, he shut the bird down and hopped out to stretch his legs.

Mark looked around and shook his head. "This guy has to be one of us. Who else would think to find a quiet place on top of a building in the middle of downtown?"

They all grinned as they looked around the city. Jack brought the conversation back to the subject. "So far we have a definite link to the operation at Don Miland's place, but additionally, we have knowledge of the nail that, we don't think John Dalman or Whitey were in on. Where does that put us?"

Laura ventured a guess, "I would think it was someone else connected to Don Miland who would know about the spiritual side of things."

Mark frowned, "You mean the demon that was Don Miland's silent partner is the one behind the attacks on us?"

She shook her head, "No, I think it has to be someone in the world, but who is privy to the spiritual side. Now, it would have to be someone with big bucks and a lot of connections, to have all those people attacking us at one time and with the gear and coordination they had."

Jack added, "That's good, and don't forget about our "creature" in the alley. That is a really strange angle. That may mean that there is another player besides the human out there targeting us."

Laura said, "We did well tonight, finding out what those guys knew. By the way, what did you do with those three guys?"

Jack answered, "We waited until the truth serum was ineffectual and then used their phone with a voice modulator, to call 9-1-1 and tell them that there was a break-in at that suite and that there were injured people there."

Sara's eyebrow went up again. "Don't you think leaving witnesses around will be a problem?"

Mark laughed, "No, because Marco and the lawyer never woke up and saw us. The guy that attacked you is completely paralyzed from the neck down and can't talk. If they can bring him out of his traumatized state, he only got a short look at me in the middle of the fight, and I don't think that it will remain in his mind because he's got a lot of other things to contend with right now."

Jack smiled at Mark, "Of course you did tell him that it was your wife he attacked."

Mark thought back for a few seconds. "Oh yeah, I forgot about that. I'm not used to having loved ones on the firing line and it slipped out. But the way he looked at me there is probably more than one husband looking for him, anyway."

Sarah snuggled up to Mark and kissed him.

Major White came back and they headed back to the air field and then on to Castle Malone. Jack was quiet on the trip back and Laura picked up on it. "What's the matter?"

Jack shook his head, "I don't know, but something tonight is bugging me. Something I'm overlooking."

Laura reached out and put her hand in his. "Ask the Holy Spirit to remind you."

CHAPTER EIGHT

Jack sat up in bed. He looked at the clock on the wall. The softly glowing, four-inch tall numbers read 3:45 a.m. He got up quietly so as to not disturb Laura, and put on his robe. He padded down the cushy carpet to the upstairs guest suite. Knocking quietly on the door he waited. In a few seconds the door was opened by Mark. Resetting the safety on his pistol he tipped his head at Jack as if to say, "What?"

Jack motioned him out of the room to let Sarah sleep. After they went downstairs to the kitchen, Jack told Mark. "I've had something nagging at me since we left those guys last night. I prayed and asked the Holy Spirit to remind me and he just did. That list of people they were supposed to pick up to use as levers on us, it was a Xerox copy. That means that same list could be in other people's hands, too. We need to warn them all about this."

Mark thought for a bit. "You're right and tomorrow morning may be too late. I should have caught that." Mark frowned and sat down, "Maybe I'm getting too old for this game."

Jack laughed softly, "Yeah, sure. Mark, when you were younger, didn't you miss things? Didn't your teammates have to carry some of the load? Pick up on things? Be there for you like you were for them?"

Mark wryly smiled, "Yes, they did, and yes, I did miss things. You're right, that is a negative confession I just made and I renounce it in the name of Yahshua. I'm not getting older, I'm getting better!"

Jack smiled again, "Just don't let it go to your head. Remember, the pride thing?"

Mark stood up and gently slapped Jack on the shoulder. "Thanks for reminding me. That is a weak area I'm working on and it's the other side of negative confessions, over positive convictions."

Jack went into the den/office area of the house. He pointed Mark to the other phone and picked up his receiver and dialed out on line one. He listened to it ring for three rings and then it went into the recorder. He left a message for his dad to call him back immediately on his cell phone. He then dialed his Uncle's number. Larry Malone picked up on the second ring. "Hello?"

Jack asked to be forgiven for the early hour but that it was important. He explained what they had learned and about the list with Larry's name on it. Larry understood and was grateful for the call. He would take precautions and be on the alert for any snatch and grab operations around himself or his family. When Jack asked about his dad, Larry said that his brother was in the mountains looking for a site for his church construction and gave Jack the cell phone number.

Jack tried the cell phone but didn't get a connection. That worried him.

Using Jack's palm pilot with the numbers, Mark had contacted Carol Nolan and warned her. He had then called Sensei Grady's cell phone and managed to get him just as he was headed out for dinner, in the Orient. He said that he would take steps and offered to come back to help them, since he was in the last days of his visit. Mark welcomed the older man's offer because of his police days and his knowledge of the local crime scene in the Denver area. The Sensei said he would make arrangements for a flight tomorrow.

Jack called Minister Throman and, again, apologized for the early call but stressed the danger. The Minister thought for a minute and said that he had wanted to take a sabbatical for quite some time now and tomorrow would be a good time to start. He said that he was going back east to visit some relative and not let anybody but Jack know where he was headed. Jack agreed and hung up. Mark told him about the Sensei coming back to help them.

Jack sat there for a few minutes thinking. "I've got to go find my father or find out if they have already gotten to him. He's in the mountains somewhere, according to Uncle Larry. It may be that he's in an area where the cell phone won't work or he's turned it off, but I need to make sure. He didn't ask for this trouble and I want to see that he doesn't get hurt."

Mark agreed and said, "I think you should keep Laura with you and go well-armed in your SUV. Sarah and I will wait here for the Sensei and see what we can find out about our playmates of last night and their connections."

It was now four-thirty and Jack decided to take a shower and get things ready. He wouldn't wake Laura up until seven. Mark went back to bed.

CHAPTER NINE

As they drove through the mountains on I-70 they enjoyed the view. The Aspens were turning early this year and the colors were riotous, gold and green with the "quakies" twinkling in the sun. The combination of the autumn colors with the crisp air always cheered Jack up, regardless of what was going on. This time it didn't help. He was worried about his father, alone and possibly the target for forces unknown.

Laura noticed Jack's concern and took his hand. "Don't forget that your dad was a Christian long before you were. He walks with the Lord and right now is on a mission for the Lord. I think Yahveh will protect him and the best thing we can do is pray for him."

Jack thought about that and agreed that it was only Yahveh who could protect anybody, in reality. He relaxed and smiled at his wife. "You are a Godsend to me, know that?"

She nodded her head, "Yeah. And you are one for me, too."

They had checked with Larry again and gotten an approximate area for the site Steve was looking for, above Eagle, in the middle of the state. He told Larry that the property values were much more reasonable and it would be a better distance for travelers, than right in the middle all the ski areas closer to Denver.

They came into Eagle and stopped at the city information center right off the interstate. Finding that there are only three reputable motels in the town, they started with the best one and found where he was staying right away.

They knocked on his room door but there was no answer. Jack didn't see any cars near that area so they assumed he was up looking around the area. Laura suggested that they try the local real estate offices. They tried several and stopped for lunch. After lunch they found the real estate office he was using. He had been there that morning and left with one of the agents for a selection of sites. The office secretary called the agent on the radio and found out where they were. She showed them a map and told them how to get there. Jack was relieved that his dad was all right.

After twenty minutes of driving up mountain roads, they spotted the agent's Mercedes Benz. Pulling up behind the other car, they got out and looked around. Not seeing anyone, they decided to wait there.

Steve Malone and the agent came walking back to her car through the trees, in a few minutes. Seeing Jack and Laura he waved. Waving back, they walked out and met them halfway to the tree line.

After a hug, Steve asked, "Have you finished your business and decided to come up and help me look for a church site?"

Jack smiled, "Not really." He asked the agent if they could have a minute alone. She walked back to her car.

Jack looked at his dad and felt sorry for putting such a damper on his day, but it had to be done. He told him about the list and results of their "business" of the other day. "We're worried about you up here. I couldn't get you on the cell and was concerned that they had found a way to track you."

Steve looked around the beautiful fall mountainside. "I doubt that anyone but you could find me here. Larry is the only one that even knows remotely where I am. But I'm glad you're here. I think I'll keep looking around at sites for a while. I've actually seen one that I think will be perfect. I'm just shopping around until the Holy Spirit gives me a confirmation. It's got good access to a major road, it's not too far off the interstate, and it's got a magnificent view from a cliff top that would work very well."

Laura said, "I'd like to see it if you have time."

Steve looked at Jack to see if he had any objections. He didn't.

"Okay, let's go. I'll ride with Ms. Wiggons and you guys follow us."

They got into the cars, made a careful U-turn and headed back towards Eagle. About a half of a mile from the descent into the town proper, they stopped by the side of the road and got out again. They walked about five hundred yards through the scrub brush and small trees to a cliff that looked out over a beautiful small valley. The view was to the south, so the sun was either above or on either side of the view, not directly into it. The fall foliage was colorful and it was, altogether, an excellent view.

Steve was pointing out the dimensions of the proposed building and parking lot to Jack when Ms. Wiggons let out a gasp. Spinning around they saw Laura's armor and sword in full display. She had turned around and the glare off of her armor from the high sun was enough to cause tears.

Laura had felt the anointing of the Holy Spirit and had started to pray in tongues as she turned towards the road. An indistinct darkness hovered near the ground close to them.

Laura said to them in a voice that did not brook any resistance, "Get back, now!" Ms. Wiggons didn't know what to do so Jack pulled her behind him, as they moved behind Laura.

Jack was asking the Lord what the best thing to do would be, when Steve Malone said, "Look, over on the road."

Laura was advancing on the darkness with her sword. Her concentration was totally on the odd blackness. That evil spirit feinted as it moved towards her and got larger and more solid. It began to look like a demon rather than a poor drawing of a rain cloud. It wasn't interested in Laura but was attempting to get past her to where Jack was standing.

Laura started reciting the 23rd Psalm, *"Yea though I walk through the valley of death I shall fear no evil for you are with me. Your rod and your staff ..."*

In response to the prayer the light from the sword grew in intensity so that it rivaled the sun. The demon/blackness recoiled from the light and started moving away from Laura as the light reached for it. The darkness suddenly seemed to flee into the distance and disappeared.

Laura felt her armor fade out and she turned to find Jack right next to her almost picking her up as all of them ran towards the woods on the mountainside. The beautiful scenery and dappled sunlight under the trees seemed at terrible odds to the serious headlong rush they were making through the trees.

Jack suddenly came to a halt and pulled Laura down to the ground with himself. She looked behind her and saw that Steve had Ms. Wiggons in tow and they were down too. Looking to their left, she made out several armed men heading towards the cliff where they had been. The men didn't see the four people crouched in the low scrub in the trees.

After the men had passed, they took off again and approached their cars. The enemy had left a guard who was trying to break into the SUV with no success. Jack quickly closed with the man before he knew they were there. At the last second the man saw Jack's reflection and whirled around. He stabbed at Jack with the knife he had been using on the car.

Jack countered the thrust with his left hand, slapping the knife hand to the right and between them and then crashed into the man at full speed, driving him into the side of the SUV. The smaller man gasped at the collision and crumpled to the ground. Jack stepped back in guard position, ready for the thug's next move, but he didn't expect it to be massive bleeding. The knife had gotten wedged between them when they hit and had been driven deeply into the man's chest just below his heart. Well, maybe not too much below the heart, judging by the copious amount of blood he was leaking.

Jack squatted down and asked him, "Who sent you to attack us?"

The man seemed to know he wasn't going to make it. He looked at Jack and said, "Gregory DeMeers paid us to kill Steve Malone and make sure that there were no witnesses." The man's eyes got bigger and he pawed at Jack, whispering, "Help meeee!"

Jack wanted to ask where this Gregory DeMeers was but it would have been a wasted question. The man's eyes lost their animation and his head lolled to the side as he let out a last sigh.

Laura came up to Jack as he closed the man's eyes and laid him down on the ground. He looked at her and asked, "Did you know your armor would go away after that demonic spirit left?"

She shook her head, "Nope."

Steve Malone was attempting to calm Ms. Wiggons down and pull the cockle-burrs off her skirt. By the time they got back to her car, out of the sight of the carnage, she was somewhat coherent and almost calm.

Steve looked at her. "I'm sorry that happened while you were with us. But it did accomplish one good thing for you."

She looked up in surprise as if there could be any good thing come out of the recent action.

He said, "That was sufficient confirmation for me. I'll take the property."

That perked her up, considering the large bonus she would get on top of her commission.

Jack got Steve and Ms. Wiggons into her car and off for town and then he and Laura took the SUV and drove down to the attacker's vehicle. Powering down his window, Jack shot out both tires on that side of the car. They then sped away as the men ran out from the trees, yelling and shooting.

After they reached town they went to the police. The police sent a cruiser up to the property to check out the area. While they were waiting to find out what the police found, they made out the reports. The police at the scene found the dead man and the disabled car but couldn't find any sign of the other men. They went through the vehicle the attackers apparently came in and found the rental slip and called in the credit card and number used to rent it. Jack copied the information down, and would have Sensei Grady check that out, when they got back home.

Laura talked to Sally, as Ms. Wiggons turned out to be, and tried to explain what happened. Sally wasn't religious and didn't understand the armor or the darkness she had seen, but she was willing to accept that the bad guys had been outfoxed and the good guys had won. She also decided to ask her boss for hazardous duty pay for this particular trip.

In the end, the Sheriff agreed to see if he could find out who the unidentifiable attackers were, since the dead man did not have any identification on him and Jack's group couldn't identify any of them. Jack, Laura, and Steve had to sign papers agreeing to stay where they could be found during the investigation. The Sheriff didn't know whether to be glad or not, when he found out that Steve Malone was purchasing property in his county.

As Jack drove his dad back to his car at the agency, Steve shook his head, "So, you meant it when you said they were aggressively seeking your Treasure and the elimination of anyone else involved. I'd say that was a fairly good validation."

Steve frowned, "How is it possible they missed us if they are in league with the devil? He had to know where we were."

Laura piped up, "Maybe the two groups don't communicate. You know? Different groups with the same orders."

That was something to think about.

Jack's cell phone rang and he answered it. Minister Throman was back in town and wanted to get together as soon as possible. He indicated it was urgent. Steve signed an agreement to have his lawyer check out the property and deeds and purchase agreements. He then decided to go back to Denver with Jack and Laura. He parked his car behind the real estate agency, with their permission, and rode back in the SUV. Somehow he felt safer doing that.

CHAPTER TEN

Sensei Jim Grady exited the aircraft disembarking tube and looked carefully around. He was definitely on alert. He started for the terminal and the baggage area when he saw Mark and Sarah standing there. They had seen him but were scanning the crowd of passengers rather than having a royal welcoming.

He walked by them and winked and kept walking. They followed him at a reasonable distance while keeping the people around him, and them, under surveillance. They continued that way to the baggage claim area. He waited for his bag and casually leaned back against a pillar. Mark noted that this limited the approaches to him to the front. His teacher was still very smart.

The baggage arrived and his bags came up together. He waited until they were both close to where he was and then he stepped forward and picked them both up. Walking to the exit he showed his tags to the police officer standing there. He headed on out towards the parking area. Mark and Sarah closed up on him and were two people behind him when the action started. Two men jumped out of a large sedan parked at the curb. Both of them had handguns out. Mark yelled loud enough for people in the parking structure to hear him. "Federal Agents, everybody down now!"

It was heartening to see the majority of the people drop to the pavement. Sarah had a Tel Aviv flashback. The two gunmen, who were suddenly exposed, turned their guns towards Mark. Mark had already marked the left hand man and squeezed off a shot. Sarah matched him with the man on the right. The Tazers worked excellently while not threatening anyone else. Both men dropped their guns and started jerking and then fell to the ground. Just then the window on the back seat of the sedan rolled down and a shotgun barrel extended out of it. Mark threw himself to the left, Sarah went right. The shotgun roared and the buckshot took out the major pane of glass behind where Mark had been standing.

A glint of light flew into the back of the sedan and the shotgun disappeared. The car roared to life and sped away. Sirens were screaming everywhere as the police rapid response team came to the scene. The car was cut off and run into the railing on the left hand side of the ramp. The police closed in on the car and ordered the driver out with his hands up. He didn't listen to them because he was too busy doing something in the car. Sarah took an educated guess and yelled, "Bomb! Get away from the car, Bomb!" The police scattered like leaves in the wind. Two heartbeats later the car exploded and opened up like a tin can with a cherry bomb going off inside.

As the parts of the car finished dropping to the ground, men started showing up with FBI on their vests. Very heavily armed and looking for any excuse to use their weapons.

Mark put his Justice Department badge on his jacket pocket and holstered his gun. Sarah did the same. They walked over through the crowd that was tentatively rising from the ground. The Sensei stood there and frowned. "They don't care who they hurt or kill, do they?"

Sarah mumbled something about militants and terrorists being one and the same thing. The she smiled to the older man, "I would say you've had a warm welcome home."

About that time one of the senior FBI agents collared Mark and Sarah and started demanding information. Mark looked at him for a second and then took out his cell phone and made a call. The FBI agent looked like he wanted to rip the phone out of Mark's hand when his cell phone started ringing. He ripped it out, flipped up the handset and yelled, "What!?"

He started deflating immediately and just kept getting smaller until he hung up. Looking at Mark with a brand new attitude he asked if they would be inclined to help him with the case. Mark nodded and walked off with him leaving Sarah to take care of the Sensei, not that he needed help. Mark knew that glint of light going into the back of the car would have been a very accurately aimed Chinese throwing star most recently in the hand of Jim Grady.

After they dictated their statements and left the airport, Jim Grady was telling them how glad he was that they had decided to meet him at the flight.

Mark was concerned about something else though. "How did they know that you were on that flight? You wouldn't use your real name,"

The Sensei looked at his former student like he had lost his limited amount of intelligence. "Of course I did not. I used a fabricated name."

"Then how did they know you were coming in?"

Sarah suggested a different thought, "Maybe they were just watching for anybody and saw him."

Mark shook his head as he veered around a slower truck. "I hope not, because that would indicate they have a lot of men if they can just plant some at the airport in the off chance they'll see someone they want."

CHAPTER ELEVEN

Jack and Laura went to southeast Littleton to see the Minister in response to his call.

After greeting them at the door, the Minister had them come in and he shut the door. The three of them sat around the table in comfortable chairs.

Minister Throman started out explaining why he had come back so quickly from his trip. "I know that you wanted to keep me safe by keeping me out of here, but this is too important to leave to a phone call. I have been praying about your question concerning the nail. I think I understand now about the Holy Treasure that you guard for the Lord. By itself it is nothing more than a piece of metal. But I believe I was shown that all material things retain a connection in the spiritual realm to any spiritual energy that is released near them.

Anyway, the closer to the energy and the more solid the object, the longer it will retain the connection to the spiritual energy patterns impressed on it. The more intense the spiritual pressure or stress, the more energy is etched into the fabric of the object. Think about anointed cloths as an example.

There hasn't been any event on Earth to rival the crucifixion of the Lord as far as release of spiritual energy is concerned. Think of the energy involved when all the sins of the world were poured onto Jesus as He hung on the cross. Hundreds of years after the event, Saint Catherine found that the wood of the cross retained enough energy to heal sickness in a person. Wood is very porous compared to iron in the spiritual realm as far as retaining spiritual energy.

I also think because of the continual warfare by the enemy to obtain the nail, the faith and sacrifice of the Christians defending the nail and the close contact it had with the spiritual force of the Lord during the stress of the crucifixion, the energy level connected to the nail has probably increased rather than decreased over the millennia. If Satan can acquire it, he can use its spiritual force in ways we don't understand yet to mask or possibly amplify evil. This is why the nail cannot be allowed to fall into his hands.

But I also don't think that is our greatest worry. The Lord showed me a vision that has concerned me for the last two nights. I have prayed for understanding concerning this and I don't like where these thoughts are taking me.

There are men seeking the nail for its spiritual energy also. They intend to use it allow one of their own to perform miracles similar to those performed by the Apostles. Whatever they intend to use this for it is a base reason with horrific results. I saw thousands upon thousands of Christians under heavy bondage and suffering by these men's hands. They are powerful now and will seek greater power but I don't think any of them is the anti-Christ yet. It is possibly a precursor or shadow of his, but, not the actual one. Unfortunately, I saw the attempted destruction of Israel by this group also.

This group will not be denied in their desire to possess the nail. As long as they are alive they will do everything within their power to possess it."

Jack asked, "If Yahveh gave you a vision of the destruction, bondage, and suffering is it a fact that these things will happen?"

Minister Throman shook his head. "No, I don't think so. I think it is a possible future if they aren't thwarted in their desires to possess the nail and the energy it is connected to today."

Laura was quiet as she listened to the description of their enemy. "If they are already powerful then they should be locatable too. Do you have any other clues as to who these people are?"

The Minister shook his head. "No, unfortunately I don't. But I feel sure that the Lord will reveal their identity to you when He is ready. Until then, do the best you can with what you have."

There was some noise in the adjoining room and the Minister got up to see what was going on. Jack was thinking about what he had said and looked up to see him look out the window.

Three men looked at the Christian Church from the parking lot. They moved to the front door of the church.

It was open and they walked in. Seeing a sign indicating the church offices they went into the secretary's area. No one was there. They walked quietly down the carpeted hall to the Minister's office. The door was closed and locked. All three men drew silenced weapons and on the count of three they kicked in the door and went in shooting.

Jack got up and looked out the door.

The phone rang and the Minister answered it and listened for a few seconds. Hanging up he looked at Jack. "You were right. One of the elders just called to say some men broke into my office and shot it up with silenced handguns.

Even though Minister Throman was in his late seventies he was coping well with the constant danger. He frowned and sat back down.

The Minister finished praying for his church and against the evil done there. He looked at the two of them and smiled. "I just knew after that baptism that my life was going to be exciting whenever you guys are around. I want you to know that I have been blessed more than ever before in my life since I've met you."

Jack smiled back, "I'll bet you've never had your office shot up before you met us either."

"True, true, but I have drawn close to the Lord in the months since your baptism and I believe I finally met the Lord in prayer the other day. He told me that I was blessed in His service and that He would protect me from these men. I guess I don't have to go on that sabbatical again."

Jack thanked him for everything and the two of them turned to leave the motel where they had met. "I would think you could probably still do with a short leave of absence. At least until this thing is over."

The Minister thought that Jack might have a point there. The Lord would protect him but it wasn't right for him to knowingly walk in harm's way just because he was protected.

CHAPTER TWELVE

Jack was sitting at home, watching his wife. Laura was reading her Bible and being comfortable in her skin as the trendy people would say. She had just had a shower and was curled up in her favorite nightgown and robe in her favorite soft chair with the light just behind her.

Jack thought again how much he loved her and was pleased that she wasn't in the middle of war zone at the minute. He realized that she had changed since their wedding. She had become softer and harder at the same time. Her love for the Lord humbled her but her warfare in the real world and the spiritual one had given her a confidence she did not have when they were wed. Of course that could be said of either one of them.

He then realized that for Mark and Sarah their lives were about the same considering that she was an ex-Mossad agent and he was a top counter-terrorism expert and an ex-Navy SEAL. This latest spate of attacks had brought them all together in ways they hadn't known before. He was pleased with the closeness between them and the Connelly's and between all four of them and the Lord.

He sat back and considered the fact that it had been over two weeks since the last attack. That was the one on the Minister's office. The names they had gotten were just low-level organizers who were dead or missing. The whole thing had led to a series of dead ends. Jack wasn't dim enough to think that they were the ones behind the attacks or that the business with the nail was over. No, it implied that the power behind the attacks were smart enough to hide their presence completely. That spoke of power, money, and a high level of sneakiness.

The craftsmen had come and gone and the house looked like nothing had happened to it. Two additional things had been done though. Jack and Mark had designed a floor mounted secure safe for the keeping of the nail. It was definitely a secure safe. The way the craftsmen installed it, the whole house would have to be destroyed just to get to it. Then it would take a considerably talented computer safe cracker to break into the vault. If it came to that though, their time would be wasted. The magnesium fire would see to that. The team had come to the decision after Jack had asked them if the nail would be better destroyed than to let it fall into the hands of either the enemy of mankind or his lesser ilk. The design was a takeoff of one of his father's safe houses. It was a complex yet simple design that would require either Laura or him to open it correctly. To open it correctly they couldn't be under stress or duress. Anything but the correct procedure for opening the safe would result in the instant destruction of Yahveh's treasure.

The other new thing was a very much more secure garage and parking area.

It was close to eleven p.m. when the NovaStar system announced a visitor. Jack turned on the TV and examined the caller from three angles. It looked like a messenger and there were no ferrous objects large enough to be a gun. Jack got up and bounced down the stairs in a loose shirt and jeans. He was shoeless but with his training that was the natural way he fought anyway. He used the intercom to determine that it was a letter for him. He opened the door and took the letter from the man and signed the wireless record log. Closing the door he watched the man leave the building and get into his car.

Jack carried the letter into the den and ran it through a series of tests in a specially designed machine. The package was inert and did not show signs of any pathogen or disease. It was what it said it was as far as the low-level x-ray scan was concerned, no wires or connectors. He took it out of the machine and opened it. Inside was an elegant invitation.

He reread the invitation twice as he carried it back upstairs to the master bedroom. He looked at the door to Mark and Sarah's room and didn't see any light at the bottom. They had been working hard to track the attackers and needed their sleep.

Laura looked up at him when he returned. He handed her the invitation and watched her face as she read it. Both eyebrows went up and she compressed her lips. This was high praise indeed for the small piece of paper in her hands.

"What do you think about that?" His question to her was a testing of the waters. She looked up at him and said, "Okay, he is one of the richest men in the world. His charities and food programs have fed millions for free. He runs some of the largest food conglomerates that have ever existed. We have no connection on any level with him. Why? Why us? Why now? For... what reason?"

Jack didn't have any answers, yet. The invitation was from Victor Tyrone Chamberlain. In personal wealth alone he was worth somewhere in the area of thirty billion dollars. The invitation asked Jack and Laura to visit him at his home on his South Pacific island in three days. It stipulated that there was an important thing that the three of them needed to discuss. All well and good except for three major hurtles. First, Victor Tyrone was a very private person. He would be considered an eccentric recluse for someone in the higher tax brackets. Nobody saw him or ever visited his island. There were no pictures of him or his island except at extreme long range. Paparazzi knew enough to not try to approach the island, it wasn't healthy.

Second, his recently discovered dislike for anyone who professed a religion. Word had leaked out that he was an equal opportunity "Disliker" though. He did not like people who were Christian, Jewish, Muslim, Buddhist, Hare Krishna, or any other form of (as he put it) gutless dependence on a "higher power".

Thirdly, was a widely-distributed rumor of an attitude of dislike for anything "American", especially anyone who had been financially successful in the U.S. Apparently he felt they were the biggest abusers of the world's poor in the entire world.

Actually, there was a fourth problem with the invitation. He had expressly invited Laura, yet whispers had run the circles for years about his avoidance of anything having to do with the distaff side of humanity. Apparently his rejection of womanhood was so complete that it was legend. It was said that he so disliked women that he couldn't possibly have had a mother, he just spontaneously appeared on the scene, bypassing the entire female birth process which he deemed as unworthy of one such as himself.

Jack didn't know whether to believe the rumors or not but a great deal of the world's population seemed to have that image of the man so there was probably some truth in them.

Jack computed the time difference and put in an international call to Israel. He got hold of David Zahavy after several delays. David had been a friend and fellow soldier in the battle against the Arab Strike Force several months ago and was a personal friend of Sarah's as well as her ex-boss.

"David! How are you doing?" Jack's greeting was upbeat and casual. David wasn't deceived at all, possibly one of the reasons he was one of the top agents of the Mossad. "Jack, I'm fine, what's wrong?" Straight to the point like usual.

"David, I've got a situation I would like your advice on. My wife and I just got an invitation to Victor Chamberlain's island for talks. I don't understand it in the light of his views on Americans, women, and religion. Can you tell me anything about him that would make sense of this?"

David whistled, "Wow, that's a rare thing you've got there. See if you can get me some of his napkins or silverware, huh?"

"Sure, I'll try to get you his unlisted phone number too."

David laughed. "Okay, let me look into this and I'll give you a call, in about, say, eight hours, or will that give you enough sleep? Oh! I'm also going to send you a package."

Jack chuckled, "We'll be waiting for your call. I'm sure Sarah will want to talk to you then."

They hung up and Jack stretched. It was time for some sleep.

CHAPTER THIRTEEN

The demon authority cast about to find an upper level demon that he could use in this case. He located a particularly nasty survivor that showed some promise for leadership. He called that demon in front of him and gave him the instructions on how to handle the action about to transpire on Chamberlain's island. He was very explicit. There could be no mistakes this time. There were too many chances that the prize could be lost forever. The Malones were not to be allowed to succeed at their game. They were to give up possession of the nail. All hell would pay if they didn't give it to the Master's men on the island!

At ten-thirty in the morning the phone rang and Laura answered it. "Hello? David! How are you?"

David laughed, "You guys ask that like you really care. But then, you do care don't you? Anyway, I need to talk to both of you and Sarah and what's-his-name."

Laura laughed and called the others over to the table. She hit the speaker button and announced, "Okay, Jack, Sarah, and what's-his-name are here."

Mark made a surprised looking face and pointed at himself and mimed "Who, me?"

Everyone laughed at that. Mark spoke up, "Hey, what's-his-name has a name too you know."

David shot back, "Oh, really? Which name are you using at this time, Mr. Rosen?" That was an alias that Mark had used in Israel in the past.

"Why don't we use Mark for the time being."

David turned serious at that point. "Okay Mark, listen up. We did an in-depth research of Victor Chamberlain and you will be interested in our results."

Mark said, "Wait one." He flipped the switch that activated the built-in solid state memory to record the call. The "beep" that sounded every fifteen seconds wasn't too intrusive but let the caller know that the call was being recorded.

David launched into his report. "First of all, let me say that the saying that money corrupts and ultimate money corrupts ultimately seems to apply in this case. Victor Chamberlain is a very good example although you'd never know it through the public media. He seems to be philanthropist and an exceptionally concerned sponsor of the poor and destitute. Our recent investigations make that seem to be a carefully designed image that he maintains. From what we can determine, at least recently, he actually doesn't care or like the downtrodden except where they can be used."

Laura broke in, "What about all his charities and free food for the starving of the world that are constantly in the news? Are they real?"

"Well, the events and the charities are real. But, we think that they are staged events to garner the best image available. The truth is that his companies make several grades of food. The lowest grade is called "basic" and is rather unpalatable for all but a person who is really starving. Like most food manufacturers, we think Chamberlain's industries make the most profit off of the cheapest foods and therefore they push the least nutritious but most profitable brand the hardest. What he can't sell after a reasonable amount of "shelf" life, he is supposed to throw away as unfit. Rather than do that, his companies make a big media show of handing out the food to the people who would never complain about it regardless of how old and moldy it is. They really are starving and it is a service but it's like a freebie throw-away that they make out to look like they are magnanimously giving quality food to poor people. The sad part is that people still starve eating his hand outs because there is so little nutritional value in the food that they don't gain anything but minimal calories and indigestible bulk from eating it."

Sarah chimed in, "That's horrible but it doesn't track with the history of his food for the poor operation. While I was with the Mossad I was tasked with doing an in-depth report on his operations and their relationship to Israel."

She glared at the speakerphone. "You should remember it because you assigned me to it. Pull it up and look at it. Over a ten year period he sent tons of food to dozens of starving populations and the reports showed that he was actually preventing wide-spread starvation. The UN did hundreds of spot checks of the food eight years ago and rated it excellent. If it is as bad as you tell us, why hasn't some recent news outlet exposed them?"

David laughed, "Oh yeah, sure, who's going to take after a powerhouse like Chamberlain and his controlling investments in the news industry? It would be like chewing on the hand that feeds you. They don't dare point a finger at him or they get cut off from the money trough."

Mark followed another track. "What did you mean by absolute corruption?"

"You remember what happened to Howard Hughes? How he went insane and his advisors kept him isolated until he finally died? Well, this could be a similar case even though we think the principal is still functioning. He could be losing it which would explain the changes in his image."

David continued reading aloud, "Our recent investigation suggests that Chamberlain is certifiable right now. He has an extreme messianic complex coupled with more money than Midas and a group of toadies that apparently feed him whatever he wants to hear so that they don't lose their lucrative jobs. The entire staff is loyal to a fault and unwilling to provide input regardless of the incentive"

David continued, "Actually, we are not sure who is in control there. It could still be Chamberlain but it might not be. It is very hard to determine from the outside and they are an in-bred group that will not tolerate outsiders. It is confusing because this goes against everything we think we know about this man. This invitation to Jack and Laura is an opportunity that hasn't existed for the last fifteen years."

Jack said, "That doesn't make it worth the danger to Laura and me to accept the invitation. Let's face it. The only thing I have that he can't get anywhere else is the crucifixion nail. It follows that he will make an offer that will include my, her, or our safety as a requirement to deliver it to him. I won't do that unless Yahveh tells me to. If he is demented then the whole thing will be a carefully orchestrated affair by him or his handlers. Either way I don't think the chance to look into his private life is worth the risk."

David agreed with him. "You're right that it wouldn't be worth it just for the inside information on him. That's not the problem. The problem is that we think he has been involved recently in deep cover funding and supply for an extremely nasty terrorist group you and I have had business with lately. Remember the ASF? The group that tried to poison the world and was supposedly hunted out of existence by the Mossad and the United States Military just a few months ago? We now have reliable information that the real mastermind for that operation is probably secluded on Chamberlain's island and is working with him for a rebirth of the organization under a new name but with the same goals."

Jack's eyebrows rose slightly. "If this is supposed to be an incentive for me to put Laura and myself at risk it isn't helping. The ASF has a particular hatred for us. If the real head of the snake is there, why do we want to put our heads in his mouth?"

David sighed, "None, really. I understand your reluctance and actually I approve of your caution. It would be worth the Intel if the danger wasn't so real. We'll keep an eye on him but I doubt that your refusal to come to him will be the end of his efforts to get what he wants."

"True", Jack agreed, "But he, if it was him, has tried to get it by force and was unable to acquire it. Now he's trying diplomacy. What's left?"

David sighed again, "I don't know, and that's what worries me. I genuinely love you guys and don't want to see any harm come your way. Keep us in mind if you rub shoulders with him or his guys again. Maybe the time will come to ignore the politicians and go for a full scale raid on his island."

They hung up and discussed the situation.

Laura suggested that it looked like another victory for Satan. The lofty world image, the rip-off of the food programs, all the drastic change.

It didn't look promising to consider a trip to Chamberlain's island.

CHAPTER FOURTEEN

The rest of the day the team split up. Laura and Sarah worked on attempting to track down the whereabouts of the people the Malones had been involved with at the time of their original Don Miland episode. The one person that they were interested the most in was Whitey, the criminal break-in artist who had slipped away from police observation during the climax of the confrontation with Don Miland. They were making some headway as there were rumors of his being in various places at different times since then. Sarah's Mossad training and Mark's security contacts were just about at their limits and Laura decided to contact a friend at the Colorado Bureau of Investigation.

At the same time, Jack and Mark took a trip to a local food processing plant in Colorado Springs which was owned by Chamberlain Industries. They posed as interested businessmen who were looking for contracts to supply a workforce numbering several thousand. As prospective clients they were shown everything that the plant could produce and even given samples of each type of food which were surprisingly good. The pricing and distribution schemes were brilliant and very competitive with any other form of supply. Both men came away from the probe with a definite impression of professionalism and quality that was at direct odds with what David's investigation seemed to show. They discussed the obvious discrepancy as they drove back to the house.

Jack pointed out the good manufacturing practices and quality control as leading edge management policy. Mark thought about the whole thing and came to a decision. "There is something wrong with the picture the Mossad has painted. The amount of effort to make an operation this huge work like it is doing doesn't jibe with poor quality foods and tainted supplies."

Mark added, "Maybe this plant is representative of the American operation and what the Mossad is seeing is overseas?"

Jack nodded, "That could be it. We can't tell until we check it out by going over there. Still, David and his people don't make casual mistakes. I think he is seeing something different than what we have seen today."

They drove through the NovaStar screening to park in the secure garage. After the attack on the house, Jack added some elements of the Mossad security arrangements they had encountered in Tel Aviv to his home. It had required some skilled craftsmen, some redesign of the back of the house and yard, and a pot full of money. But the results were satisfying in the additional protection it provided. The car was electronically scanned for tracking devices, bombs, or other unusual additions to the vehicle while the passengers were scanned by camera and biometric measuring sensors. Jack eyed the rapid fire AEGIS cannon mounted over the drive in an explosion-proof housing. He remembered what a similar one had done in Tel Aviv.

They walked to the house and Mark noted that the new design shut off the whole back of the house from sniper fire or rushing attack. It was impressive in that it still didn't look like a fort but like a conservative dwelling.

The two groups compared notes and listened to the war drums being sounded about the support of two terrorist groups in the Sudan on the TV while they had dinner. That night, as they slept, Jack had a dream.

The unusual thing about this dream was its extreme life-likeness. He honestly couldn't tell if he was dreaming or was awake. In fact, he forgot that he had gone to sleep and was wondering how he had come to be standing near the Pacific Ocean. The fact that the ocean was hundreds of miles from Denver didn't seem to matter.

He noticed that Laura was there with him and she was definitely not dream-like. She looked at him and nodded like she also knew something was up.

He looked to the north and saw two angels standing there. He and Laura walked over to the angels and stopped. Jack recognized Caleb the Archangel and Rose, the angel that Laura had been involved with recently.

The angels watched them approach and Caleb moved closer to them. Jack couldn't determine how he was moving, just that he approached.

Caleb smiled at them. "How are you holding up to the rigors of spiritual warfare?" he asked.

Jack motioned with his hand to Laura. "She's doing all the spiritual combat right now. I seem to be involved in the more fleshy side of the battles."

Rose had moved over to Laura's side of the little group. Her voice was a solid contralto that vibrated in one's spirit. "Laura, you have performed well."

Laura smiled, "Thanks mostly to the armor and sword you gave me. I just don't understand when it will appear or disappear and that leaves me a little uncertain as to my capabilities."

Rose nodded, "Yes, remember that the armor is a special gift from Yahveh. While it is symbolic of your protection in the Lord it is real in the spiritual world. It is a divine gift that spans the spiritual and physical worlds. You can hurt or kill a human being with your sword. If they have a demon with them you can destroy the demon with it. Because demons control many of the unsaved their reaction of fear to your armor and sword are similar. When you step out to come against a human that is driven by the enemy, a fallen angel or spiritual foe, the armor becomes effective. The sword is a physical representation of the power of Yahveh's word. As you pray to bring down strongholds and cadres, let alone a single enemy, the sword is a spiritual extension of those prayers. You will become more accustomed to the operation of your armor as you continue to challenge the evil one's emissaries. I have noticed that you are praying in the spirit continually while the armor is visible. The enemy notices your spiritual drive. They are aware of your capabilities and the threat that the armor and the sword possess, but what they aren't sure of is your commitment. I know that the Lord has given you the power and authority to overcome their efforts in every case, so be of good cheer."

The breeze was light and refreshing on the cliff top and the light was warm and softly pleasant. Everything seemed serene and Jack marveled at the peace in his spirit at this meeting. It was like the whole world was in harmony and that nothing could go wrong. There was such a sense of potential and promise of an exciting and fantastic future he couldn't help but stand in awe. He noticed that absolutely everything worked perfectly in the area of the angels. This soothed his spirit and gave him a solid clue as to understanding whether or not an angel was of the Lord. When there was confusion and chaos and disorder it was not of the Lord but of the enemy.

He asked, "Caleb, you know our present situation with the attacks and this new invitation. Can you tell me if Victor Chamberlain is the man behind all this? Also, is the invitation to his island a trap?" Jack felt at ease asking these types of question to the powerful angel because of their time together during the battle with the Omniscience Temple.

Caleb smiled again. "You are focused properly Jack. We'll have to do lunch again soon." They both laughed. "Victor Chamberlain's organization is your enemy. The man is a brilliant, well-meaning man, who chooses to be misled by his ease of success and his wealth. His future is very important to Yahveh. But the real problem is the people that are in control of his operations. They are also interacting with demonic forces that are intent on acquiring the crucifixion nail. But stand firm against them and you will prevail. You and Laura will be in danger and you both will stand in the doorway between life and death. But, hold on to your faith in Yahveh and you will achieve that which the Master has set before you."

Jack considered these words. "Can't you destroy them? Yahveh is the source of all power and nothing can stand against Him, right?"

Caleb frowned, "Yes, it is true that they get their power and life from Yahveh. But they have chosen to use that power in a completely corrupt manner. Yahveh established rules for the conflict which you call spiritual warfare. If the Lord arbitrarily wiped them out he would be deciding human fate and removing man's right to choose. If he did that in this case, where would he stop? He would have to do the same to every evil on the planet. In doing that, He would be violating His own character, which He will not do. This is a human development that Yahveh depends on his people here on earth to resolve. That is why we are meeting with you now."

Rose darkened in color. "You and Laura have been obedient and faithful to do as Yahveh has directed. He is proud of you and has great plans for your service. You are to accept the invitation to Victor Chamberlain's island and go, bringing both Yahveh's love and His wrath to that place."

Caleb reached out and touched both of them with his hands. "The anointing of the Lord is upon you to free the captives and to break bondages, tear down strongholds, preach the good news of the gospel, and to bring light amid the darkness. We will be there with you as much as we are needed. Go and remember that Yahveh has put the entire assembly of the enemy in your territory under your feet."

As they prepared to leave, Jack asked, "Should I take the crucifixion nail with me?" Caleb shook his head and said, "No, leave it in the safe you have created. The forces that want it are confused as to its whereabouts. This should keep them off balance until their end."

With that the angels faded out of sight. Jack turned to Laura and carefully memorized how she looked at that moment. She was literally glowing with Yahveh's anointing and she seemed full of the power of life. He looked down at his hands and noticed that he had the same glow. Jack suddenly woke up. He sat upright in bed and found Laura sitting there watching him.

She smiled in the dimness of the bedroom and reached out to hold his hand. Jack wondered if she had actually experienced the same dream he had. That concern was short lived. Laura said, "Wasn't that a wonderful place near the ocean? I would like to live there someday."

Jack felt the anointing of the Lord as a sparkling effervesce in his spirit. He sat there quietly enjoying the feeling and the peace. Eventually he said to Laura, "Honey, I guess we have an invitation to respond to. Let's give David a call, its tomorrow there anyway."

Laura stretched and grinned, "He will understand our change of heart, but I can't say that most people will. What about Mark and Sarah?"

Jack prayed about that one. The answer he got was in line with everything else he had experienced since he had become a Christian with an active relationship to the Lord of the Universe. "That will be up to them, but I think they will want to tag along."

"DUH!" was Laura's sarcastic comeback.

Jack laughed and picked up his cell phone from the table next to his side of the bed. After a few minutes he got in touch with David in Israel.

After explaining their decision and the reason behind it Jack asked David what he thought their options would be once they were there.

David said, "I was expecting your call. I was fairly sure that you were going to go based on what the Lord has been doing in your lives. I'm still envious of that relationship and am striving to get to that level myself."

Jack listened to the voice of the Holy Spirit as he replied. "David, you know that envy is a sin and you need to repent. Anyway, the call of Yahveh on your life is rock solid. Neither Laura nor I have ever been killed and brought back to life by Yahshua himself like you have. That type of relationship transcends any human effort or striving on your part. Like they say, just keep your eyes on Yahshua and listen to the voice of the Holy Spirit. He'll do all the work to bring you to the place He wants you. Just be confident in that and you will surpass everything you ever expected. My spirit tells me that you are on the narrow path to life and are walking in the fear and admonition of the Lord. You don't need to do anything else. Remember that you have to submit to the Lord, become smaller so that He can become larger."

David was silent for a short while. "All right, I see what you mean. I've got some praying to do tonight. Anyway, have you gotten the package I sent you yet?"

"No! Not yet."

"It should be there tomorrow at the latest. After you get it, give me a call, I don't care what time it is over here. Just call me, got it?"

Jack agreed and broke the connection.

CHAPTER FIFTEEN

Morning thundered into the Denver area in the form of a heavy thunderstorm. The rain and hail didn't disturb the residents of Castle Malone due to the unique construction and sound-deadening capabilities of the house but the continual lighting flashes fooled the attack circuitry of the NovaStar Defense System into thinking that it may be weapons fire. The system sounded an alarm at 6:43 a.m. that brought four heavily armed, pajama-clad people to the control center of the house which doubled in less troubled times as the den.

After determining the cause of the alarm, Jack brought up the system software and reset the triggering level of each gunfire flash to a shorter duration than most lightning flashes to prevent a reoccurrence of the false alarm. Since they were all up they decided to adjourn to the kitchen and make breakfast to start their day. Then everybody discovered that they needed to find the bathrooms first. After cleaning up and getting dressed in casual clothing they flipped a coin and Jack and Sarah got the KP duties and started making biscuits and gravy and bacon and eggs for everyone along with coffee and orange juice.

As the cooking was underway Jack got Mark and Sarah's attention. "Hey guys, how would you like a short vacation to the South Pacific?"

Mark exchanged looks with Sarah, "Would this be reconnaissance or backup?"

"It's a little of both. We are going to take Chamberlain up on his invitation and wondered if you two would like to walk into the enemy's lair with us?"

Sarah laughed, "You certainly know how to pique one's interest don't you?"

Mark thought about it for a few seconds. "I assume that you have gotten some direction on this? And, I assume that the direction comes from above, and that you have some information to tell us?"

It was Laura's turn to laugh. "Yes we did, yes we did, and yes we do. We actually had a shared dream last night and met two of our favorite angels, Caleb and Rose. They were explicit in detailing Yahveh's plans concerning our trip." She went on to tell the other two all that had transpired during their "dream" during the night.

The front door warning alert indicated a messenger and Jack repeated his efforts of the previous letter only this time it was a large package.

He returned to the kitchen and sat down to open the package from David. Remembering the Mossad director's request, he got his cell phone and called him at the office in Tel Aviv.

After establishing contact he opened the package. There were sixteen smaller packages inside. David told Jack to open one of each type. As he opened them he had Laura cradle the phone in the desk unit and activated the speaker phone function so that they could all be part of the conversation.

David explained the packages. "First the white package contains four wrist watches, two men's and two women's. These are some of the latest products of our advanced research labs. Each watch is exactly that, a very good, high quality time piece. The spy stuff is in the bands. There are four small lenses which you can see if you look carefully at the center of the band where it connects to the watch. The electronics and optics are excellent and the entire record is stored in the band until it is time to transmit it to the base unit."

The four of them studied the watches and tried them on for fit.

David continued, "Okay, now open the larger blue boxes. These are the base units. They look like plug-in electric shavers and bases for the men and depilatory units for the women. As soon as you are settled in, plug at least one of these into the house current. Since you four are so smart I'm sure you'll realize that they do a lot more than act as a base unit for the watch cameras. They monitor a lot of things through the electrical net in the building and also act as transceivers between you and the Mossad aircraft that will be passing by every day at seven in the morning and four in the afternoon. There will be a reconnaissance aircraft nearby from dusk to dawn but it is an unmanned drone and has limitations on what it can do."

He continued with the discussion of the base units. "There are no switches or anything odd about the base units. You can not cause them to do anything. It requires a signal from the aircraft before it transmits a burst that lasts for less than three hundred milliseconds. Now open the green boxes."

Jack cleared away the debris from the other packages and set a green one in front of each person. Mark looked at his and remarked, "This is just like Christmas, daddy!"

David replied over the phone setup, "That's not a nice thing to say to this very Jewish establishment." Then he laughed.

"Touché" said Mark.

Jack opened the green box and stared at the contents. "Okay, David, what is this?"

"What does it look like?" David responded on the phone.

"Well, it looks like a New King James Bible."

David mimicked a mortally wounded melodrama actor, "Oh No! Our secret is out! Whatever will we do now?"

Mark took his out, looked at it and then smelled it and then rubbed the pages between his fingers, "Ah ha, gotcha! It has a very slight but highly distinctive feel and aroma of Sematex. It's an explosive, right?"

"Very good Mark, don't you see the irony in it, the Mossad passing out Christian Bibles with an explosive impact?"

Jack looked at his and asked, "How do we use it?"

David laughed again, "Turn to the passage of John 8:32."

After they had all gotten there Laura read, *"Then you will know the truth, and the truth shall make you free."*

David made a suggestion. "Whatever you do, unless you want to eliminate an entire room, 'do not' fold that page in half and close the book. The pages on either side of that page are sensitive to the printing on the opposite side of that page. When you fold it and close the book, it starts a chemical reaction that takes exactly seven minutes to reach critical mass and detonate. You get the equivalent of two pounds of C4 explosive. Be careful how you bookmark your pages."

Jack asked, "What if we change our minds and want to stop it after we start it?"

David thought for a minute. "You can open the book and stop the reaction. But it will not start again after that. It will just be a book from then on."

Laura put down the Bible and looked at the ominous looking black packages left in the larger box. "What, pray tell are these delightful-looking last packages?"

"Those are your "get out of jail for free" cards. Actually, they are belts for each of you. They work great as belts but if you get locked away somewhere, assuming they let you keep your clothes and your belt, you can twist the buckle around three times and pull it out of the belt. There is exactly five fluid ounces of a highly corrosive acid you can squeeze out of the belt that will melt the toughest lock or chain. Try not to get shot in the belt."

After a few more comments they said goodbye to their Israeli friend and hung up.

Jack looked at the spy craft and shook his head. "If looks can deceive then I guess he's given us the tools to win the day."

Mark had been examining the belt, "Yeah, good workmanship. I think it would not be noticed unless they were on to the innovation."

Jack let out a big sigh, "Okay, I think it is time we responded to Mr. Chamberlain's summons."

CHAPTER SIXTEEN

Jack's call to the number listed on the invitation was answered by a staff member who said that there would be transportation at Denver's International Airport whenever they were ready to go. He gave him a contact number and hung up.

After making the preparations as necessary and incorporating all of David's equipment, the four of them set out for the airport. They were met in the private plane area by a crew and a representative for Chamberlain Industries.

The aide looked at the four of them and asked which of them were Mr. and Mrs. Malone. Jack identified himself and Laura. The man looked at his notes and said, "I'm sorry Mr. Malone, this invitation is only for you and your wife."

Jack nodded, "Yes, I know it is, but I insist that my friends go with us or you can forget it."

The man excused himself and made a cell phone call. After the call was done he ushered them all onto the Jet Commander and the plane left for the South Pacific.

The trip was uneventful and they landed at a private airport in Samaria, New Guinea. Upon debarking they were met by another group of Chamberlain's people. The man in charge was a whip-thin eastern European in an expensive suit and a slight accent named Boris. He asked to speak to Jack alone. When they had stepped aside the man asked, "Why are you being disrespectful to Mr. Chamberlain by insisting on additional people going with you when the invitation was only for the two of you?"

Jack was irritated that these people couldn't understand from one group to the other that his journey to the island was dependent on Mark and Sarah's accompanying them. "Boris, it seems that Mr. Chamberlain doesn't really want to see us. We are returning to the states until he feels the need to be reasonable and allow my friends to accompany us."

Boris sighed, "Mr. Malone, we try to do things the civilized way but sometimes people are too hardheaded for that approach. Let me tell you two things. You and your wife are going to see Mr. Chamberlain this afternoon and your friends are returning to the states on this plane. If you still don't understand me, let me make it crystal clear. This is a terminal flight for your two friends. Either they go back or we will bury them right here and you will still meet Mr. Chamberlain this afternoon."

Jack looked out and saw two men with submachine guns standing behind Mark and Sarah. They had the look of stone-cold killers without compunction. He knew that if he argued they would kill Mark and Sarah without hesitation. There was no argument with this situation. They were out-gunned and out-numbered four to one with an enemy that already had the drop on them.

Jack walked back to the group. He looked at Mark and Sarah. "Guys, I guess the invitation is only for Laura and me. You need to get back on the plane and head back to the states, please."

The last word sounded like pleading but was in actuality a code word.

Mark had seen the men with the guns and completely understood the situation, "Well, okay then buddy. Have a great trip and we'll be back some other time." He took Sarah by the hand and they re-boarded the aircraft which was being refueled. Several minutes later the plane taxied out and took off, headed back to the East.

Jack and Laura were escorted to a large helicopter for the short trip to the island.

As they arrived on the landing pad near the large mansion Jack marveled at the coordination of everything with the nature of the island. The landing pad was built into a small mesa-like rise and was elevated enough to prevent any of the low-lying vegetation from interfering with the landing pad. The electricity for the marker lights was apparently generated by two large solar panels and a flat turbine wind generator located in the base of the landing pad. The whole arrangement blended harmoniously into the natural setting of the area and unless you knew what it was, or there was a helicopter on it, it seemed normal for the landscape.

But the real treat was the synergism between the landscape and the mansion. It was a tour-de-force of inventive and creative forces. Everything about it worked with the land and the weather but still provided safety, comfort, and security for the people living in it. The approaches to the mansion were grassy, normal looking areas that led to wide, short, stone stairs that eventually reached a porch that surrounded the front and sides of the mansion. the porch was also natural rock and looked normal except for the man-made levelness of the entire structure.

There was glass in the doors and windows but it didn't glare and stand out because it was deeply set back into the rock facade of the building and was obviously a high-quality, non-glare variety of safety glass. The entire building was build into the face of a small rock cliff which faced the ocean. Trees and bushes were strategically placed and tended to provide afternoon shade and coolness and there were large screened in areas of the sides of the building that allowed the cool breezes off the ocean to flow through the building without the accompanying bugs and debris.

Walking through the wide front doors into a huge foyer Jack's trained eye picked out the use of the natural rock and interior plants to provide additional shade and quiet for conversation areas or places to think without being in the eye of other people using the foyer. He could see the green tubes that blended into the plants but probably provided water and nutriments to them from the ceiling or up from the floor.

The colors and tone of the furniture was tasteful and obviously expensive being in leather and, again, stone. The furniture was extremely functional but blended into the decor of the island perfectly. It was apparent that a great deal of creative thought and design went into the entire building.

Two men came out of a doorway and approached them and their escorts. The one man was a bullet-headed, heavy-set man with small eyes set deeply into the folds of flesh on his face. He resembled a human version of a porcine boar with his little eyes and large flat nose. The man's nose had clearly been broken and flattened early in his life and he had left it that way. His expression was one of guarded anger. He didn't walk but stalked through the room towards them like he was going to run over them. This was a standard ploy for a violent and controlling person.

The other man was taller and looked quite refined. His graying hair was carefully set in place and he assumed a regal appearance. The Holy Spirit leading let Jack know that this man was not Victor Chamberlain but would only act like him.

Bullet-head stopped very close to them to intimidate them and announced in a flat, course voice that his name was Ivan and the other man was Victor Chamberlain. After shaking hands with the phony Victor they were led to a small area of the foyer to discuss their business. The discussion was one-sided. Ivan bluntly announced that Mr. Chamberlain was interested in buying the unique Christian artifact called the crucifixion nail. In fact Mr. Chamberlain was determined to acquire it at any cost. Then, with a greedy look that made Ivan seem like he was about to start drooling, he asked if they had brought it with them.

Jack had enough of the bullying style and his eyes turned icy green. He smiled a dangerous smile at Ivan and slowly shook his head as if he were tempting Ivan to assault him.

Seeing the danger signs Ivan backed off and called in an aide. The aide brought two golden-colored rings with him. Ivan brought out a large handgun and pointed it at Laura. He looked at Jack and told him to sit still. The aide used a tool and opened one of the rings and then snapped it closed around Jack's neck. He repeated the operation for Laura.

The metal of the rings was cold but Jack could feel a humming coming from the collar. Ivan put his gun away and smiled. "Those collars are controlled from my security center. They have three uses. They can tell me where you are at anytime, anywhere on the island. They allow communications between the control center and yourselves. And, they can blow your head off. If you act hostile or uncooperative, I will detonate your wife's collar first. Now, where is the crucifixion nail?"

Jack's expression had not changed with his new decoration. "What in the perverted world you live in makes you think that either my wife or I are interested in accommodating you or your wishes? You've already made us enemies and now you threaten to kill us? Go ahead you won't get the nail that way. It is safe and only I can get to it. "

In one smooth motion Jack rose from his sitting position and side kicked Ivan into a large fern several feet away. He pivoted and grabbed the phony Victor in his arm with his other hand around the man's head. One jerk and he could break the man's neck.

Ivan struggled to his feet and rubbed his chest where he had been kicked. He glared at Jack and pulled out a small control box from his coat pocket. He smiled and pushed a blue button on the box. Jack said a prayer for his wife and himself and thoroughly expected to see them both die. But instead he felt the effects of a stun gun shock him through the collar and he lost all coordination of his muscles. He limply fell to the floor as several other men ran over to them. Things went dark at that point.

Jack came to still on the floor. He shook his head and looked around. He was lying on his back with his head in Laura's lap. She was stroking his face and calling quietly to him. He tried to smile but it came out poorly at first. Eventually he was able to sit up and look around. He and Laura were in a small three sided room that was pleasant enough. There was carpeting on the floor and a couple of easy chairs with a table between them in the middle of the room. There were a couple of day beds against the wall and to one side there was a bathroom with an open door. There were also vertical iron bars on the open side of the room with a video camera trained on the room from about ten feet away. It was mounted to the ceiling and had complete view of the room except for the inside of the small bathroom.

Laura helped him into one of the easy chairs and sat sideways in the other one facing him. Jack was quickly coming back to normal and Laura quietly told him what happened after he passed out. Ivan had the men bring them to this 'cell' and take everything of theirs except their watches and belts and shirts and slacks and socks and shoes. He had taken their luggage and gone through it looking for the nail without success. He had then told her that they had twenty-four hours to tell him where the nail was and how they could get it or they would regret it. He implied that the first thing they would do is have a full orgy in the area in front of the cell with Laura as the belle of the ball. In fact, Ivan wasn't too sure that he would wait the full twenty-four hours.

Jack looked at his lovely wife with great sadness because of the situation. She just quietly reminded him of how they had decided to get there in the first place. She wasn't worried about Ivan's threats. She said that they were protected by Yahveh's word.

Jack knew that but didn't understand her equanimity at the prospect of being raped and debased. She smiled wanly and reached down to the floor next to her chair. "Ivan did allow us one luxury", she said as she brought the copy of the King James Bible into view. "I think we will find comfort in the application of Yahveh's word."

Jack realized that his wife wasn't going to go quietly into the night if it came to that. He found peace at the prospect. He nodded and they sat back to see what Yahveh would do.

CHAPTER SEVENTEEN

As they sat there in their gilded cage, Jack prayed that Yahveh would show them a way out of their terrible situation. If they tried anything, they would die. If they did nothing, they would die. But, if they gave in and gave the nail to these people then they would live at the expense of betraying millions of Christians by siding with the enemy to save their lives. Jack already knew the answer to that. Laura and he would die first. Their lives were in the hands of Yahshua and it didn't matter who threatened them.

Still, he thought furiously for some solution. The communicators in their watches were useless without the base unit being set up. The acid in their belts couldn't be used without the camera seeing what they were doing. The only weapon that David had given them that had any possibility of working was the Bible and that would be a permanent solution. It would remove them from the equation but wouldn't help save anyone. As he prayed he felt the closeness of the Lord and he settled into the peace as a small boat comes into a sheltered cove in the midst of a violent storm. The hours were going by and it would soon be the time to tell them no or to fold the page in the Bible and tell them no with emphasis.

Even though he had taken care of his bathroom needs a short time ago he felt the urge to go to the bathroom. It was odd though, it wasn't the usual biological urge but a spiritual urge. He got up and felt his collar hum as he changed positions within the guardian field. It didn't go off so he continued to walk across the floor to the only place of any real privacy in the room. It was obvious that Victor Chamberlain had designed this "holding cell" because Jack was quite sure that the present rulers of this domain wouldn't have allowed even this little bit of decency.

As he walked out of the camera's range a strange thing happened. The back wall of the bathroom pivoted open and a young woman dressed in a simple shirt and jeans with tennis shoes was standing there with her finger to her lips in the universal sign for silence. He frowned somewhat but kept his silence and approached her. She was quite a bit shorter than him and motioned for him to kneel down in front of her. He looked back and saw Laura watching this little play.

The woman urgently motioned for him to kneel again. He knelt before her and she took a small device from behind her and placed the two leads of it against his collar. The collar opened up and she removed it from his neck. Jack noticed that one part of the unlocking device stayed on each open end of the collar and that they were connected by a wire lead. She then motioned for him to stand up and step into the tunnel which he did. All of this was done completely without noise.

She took the collar and closed it again and removed the unlocking device. She then gave the collar to Jack and motioned for him to hold it in the air at the height of his neck which she couldn't reach without a stool. He took it and held it up. She motioned for him to move it to the left a few inches as she looked at a small control panel next to her in the wall of the tunnel. The woman turned, smiled at him and pushed a control. Suddenly Jack was faced with himself. He realized it was some form of advanced holography but it had a realism he had never seen before in a light-projected simulation. Not only that but the collar was held in place on the hologram and as it began to move back into the bathroom the collar went with it.

Jack had the unusual experience of watching himself walk away from himself and go back to the seat he had been in and sit down. He noticed little glitches in the motion but it was a small jitter and he doubted that the camera would see them. He also realized that the motion of his doppelganger was a reversal of his walk to the bathroom but with him walking forward instead of backward. This was an impressive show of advanced software and application.

The woman motioned for Laura to do the same. Laura got up and was about to bring the Bible but the woman shook her head. Laura looked at Jack and folded the page in Chapter 8 of the book of John and closed the book and laid it on the table between the hologram of

Jack and her. She got up and walked slowly to the bathroom. The removal of the collar and animation of her image took even less time because the woman could do it all this time. After Laura's image was seated in front of the camera again the woman motioned them both back and the secret doorway closed and sealed.

The woman again motioned for silence and took off quickly down the tunnel which was lighted by a blue-green glow that Jack thought of as electroluminescent. They had traveled about a thousand yards when the word of Yahveh came to life in their cell and the tunnel shook and dust fell everywhere. The woman was terrified until Laura whispered in her ear that it was all right, it was just a little surprise they had left in the cell to cover their tracks. The woman had started shaking her head in a negative and then she stopped and thought about it. Then she smiled and motioned them to follow her again. This time they followed at a run.

Eventually they came out of the tunnel into the late afternoon daylight deep into the jungle of the island. The exit to the tunnel was a rock that pivoted silently up to let them out and then back with a simple push of the hand. It locked into place and looked and felt like a large boulder, nothing else.

The woman turned to Jack and held out her right hand. Jack shook her hand and said, "Thanks for getting us out of there and out of those collars."

She smiled and said, "You welcoom Jak. I am Celene. Come, the Gardener wants to meet you." Her broken English was actually understandable but she didn't talk again. They reached another boulder and it pivoted up the same way after she pressed on two spots simultaneously. They walked into the new tunnel and the boulder closed and locked. As it cut off the last rays of sunshine, lights came on and they went about two hundred feet and found a small conveyance that resembled a cross between a golf cart and an ore mine carrier. After they had gotten seated the car took off automatically and achieved a considerable velocity for about eight minutes. It then pulled into what resembled a railroad switch yard with dozens of the little cars parked on different tracks.

They disembarked and walked up a flight of stairs into the jungle again. But this part of the jungle had been civilized. There looked to be close to eighty dwellings built into the sides of hills and into the ground with round doors and round, open windows. It reminded Jack of the houses portrayed in the movies about the Hobbits in the Lord of the Ring series. But these were full sized doors and the people he could see moving about were normal sized people. Most were darker in skin color and shorter than the Malones.

Celene led them to one of the houses which didn't look any more impressive than any of the others. She knocked on the door and hearing a welcome she opened the door and led them into the house. A tall, robust African-American man walked in from the next room and smiled at Jack and Laura. He held out his hand and warmly shook both of theirs. He then turned to Celene and they traded about twenty words of an unknown language. Celene smiled at the couple, bowed, and left, closing the door on the way out.

The black man turned back to them and said, "Welcome, welcome fellow prisoners to my humble abode. Come on in and we will talk."

As they traveled through the house, Jack marveled at all the unique and fairly simple solutions to daily problems he saw in the dwelling. For example there was a riot of colorful plants hanging from the ceiling and set on tables and the floor. But the interesting part was a system of bamboo shoots that allowed a trickle of water to feed each and every pot. The source for the water was a counterbalanced bowl that slowly filled from another bamboo shoot from the outside, apparently from the gutter on the roof. The brilliance of the design was its simplicity and the fact that the plants, even though they were inside were only watered when it rained, just like they would be if they had been outside. The large windows and open frames let the sunlight and fresh air in for the people as well as the plants.

Another example of effective engineering working with nature rather than against it was the shade system. There were large leafed plants situated near each window on the south side where the sun would be the hottest during the noontime through the early afternoon. It was obvious that the plants would seek the sunlight because they were a variety that soaked up the direct sunlight in the jungle outside. As the sunlight got brighter and hotter the plants would swing their huge leaves over the window space to get the sunlight, effectively blocking off the direct sunlight into the room. Jack saw that the leaves were somewhat translucent thereby letting in a soft glow that was restful.

As they neared the area of some benches and sofa-looking seats Jack asked, "How long have you been relegated to the jungle, Victor?"

The black man stopped and turned around. His obviously agile mind let him continue without missing a beat even though it was a shock that this stranger could see through his defenses so quickly. "About six years now. How did you know? Almost nobody knows me or my face or even that I am black. I've never met you that I can remember, so, how did you know?"

Jack waved his hand around indicating the whole house. "You are more than a man, Victor. You are a creative storm of invention and practicality. I saw many signs of your brilliance in your house and I see them here too. The phony Victor Chamberlain was using your things but had no concept, not even a clue, of how to create anything unique like the systems in your mansion. He and his lackeys are like animals that have control of things they can't even understand let alone build on. When we walked in here I saw the same creative capacity and it was an easy conclusion. Besides, the Holy Spirit clued me in before we got to the island that I wouldn't be meeting you in the mansion as Victor Chamberlain.

"After they sat down, Chamberlain reached over and used a remote control and the top of the coffee table between them rotated around a central axis and presented a wet bar with a sink and faucet at one end. "Would you care for a cool drink?" Chamberlain asked them.

Chamberlain was excited and eager to learn about them and why they had come to the island. He wanted to know everything at once but the first question he asked was, "What was that marvelous explosion you left for the phony Chamberlain?"

Jack smiled, "A little gift from our friends. They built a bomb into a Bible and we just armed it when we left. Seven minutes later it went off. Although I don't know how much damage it did to your equipment and I apologize for that. We didn't know that you had an investment in that room."

Chamberlain clapped his hands, "No, no, that's perfectly all right. It was a better exit than the one I had prepared and will leave them less to investigate. Here, let me show you what happened." He got up and opened two doors to reveal what turned out to be a 60-inch flat-screen, high definition television.

Jack asked him, "How do you get this new technology out here?"

Victor smiled at him, "I have my people "borrow" things I need. They usually have full run of the Mansion and there are rooms my old associates don't go into very often. They will probably not miss a TV here and a computer there."

Sitting down again he used the remote and in a few seconds the view from the security camera showed the two of them sitting there when there was a bright light and everything went black. Victor played with the remote again and another view came on which was quite a way back into the mansion. The room they were in could just be seen to the far left. The explosion happened again and this time they could see that everything in the area was shattered. After the dust settled people were seen flooding into the area. Suddenly there was sound. They could discern people calling out commands and responses. Eventually the view switched to another camera in a control room where two people were watching the replay of the explosion. One of the two was the phony Victor Chamberlain. He was talking to his head of security, Ivan. Jack and Laura listened with interest to the byplay.

"##@**_%%#@, said the phony Victor. There goes our best chance to get that icon! Tell me again what happened! How did they get a bomb in there?"

Ivan ran the video over again in extreme slow motion. "There," he said, pointing at the screen, "The Bible. That's where the explosion started from. @$##@$!!! I should have taken that away from them too."

They watched it again for the umpteenth time. Ivan slammed his hand down on the counter. "Look at them! They act like there is nothing going to happen. Then boom! The explosion set off both of their collars and if the initial explosion didn't kill them the collars would have. We can't find crap in the rubble. They were vaporized. Everything in the room has collapsed. It is a total mess." He turned to the other man, "What do you want me to do?"

The imitation Victor sat there in thought for a while. "Since they are dead, the only way we can get the icon is through their friends, this Mark Connelly and his wife. Get a team to grab them. And for our sake make it a professional team. He got up and stormed out of the room.

Ivan sat there for a while and then picked up a phone. Dialing a number he waited and then told the party on the other end of the line, "Get me Boris!"

CHAPTER EIGHTEEN

After Victor turned off the TV Jack asked him, "Why don't you do something to get rid of them?"

Victor smiled a wan smile. "I can't do anything or they will kill me. They told me that I was a dead man walking. The only reason they leave me alive is in the event they need my mind or my signature. My only pleasures are here in my little village and my house. I have no control over my money, my property, my businesses, or even a way to contact anyone outside this island. If I were to attempt to leave or to resist these fiends I would be killed and all these gentle people would be slaughtered."

Jack watched as he talked. While he saw several different serious emotions reflected in the billionaire's face and eyes, overriding it all he saw great fear there. Jack prayed and asked the Holy Spirit what to do. He was reminded of Caleb's words. *"You are to... go, bringing both Yahveh's love and His wrath to that place."* It didn't seem like the time for wrath so it must be time for Yahveh's love.

Jack looked directly at him, "How much of the image we know outside this island is really you? Do you despise women? I don't think so because of the pleasant way you treated and talked to our rescuer, Celene. Do you ridicule religion? What is the real story behind the facade?"

Victor's face showed a monumental frown. "Lies, all lies! I have never disrespected a woman in my life. I've loved some from afar, several personally, I even married once and that was the happiest six months of my life until her untimely death. I've never had a reason to seek religion but I don't put other people down because they do. There has to be some place to put your faith and most people don't have the talent and resources that I do. They desperately need a savior. I have never needed one because I could have, do, or build anything I needed. But I don't despise any person for anything. Unfortunately that is why I am here in the jungle away from my estate.

I couldn't stand up to those men when they came against me. My servants, supposed friends, and advisors. I gave them what they wanted as long as it was reasonable. But they wanted it all. Now, even though they are my enemies they have it all and I am powerless. Without control of my wealth I am unable to do anything about the situation."

Jack smiled, "Let me tell you about my friend Yahshua."

Victor looked around his house. "I definitely have time to listen. In fact, I probably have the rest of my life."

Jack and Victor Chamberlain thought very much alike. They both had agile minds that felt they could conquer anything if they could get their mind around it. Jack had been taken to the depths by his enemies before he turned to Yahshua to save his wife. He saw great parallels with what was happening with Victor. "First, let me describe a hypothetical situation where there is a God that created the universe and everything in it. Can you work with that concept?"

Victor thought for a few minutes and nodded.

Jack remembered clearly the conversation he once had with Minister Throman before he came to know the Lord. It had been a very convincing discussion for him and he saw no reason not to present it to Victor.

He postulated Yahveh, Satan, Adam, Yahshua, and man to the black man and watched as he put the concepts together. Then Victor started asking questions. Jack, and occasionally Laura, quietly answered every question that they could from their own knowledge and in many cases, their own personal experiences.

After it had gotten dark outside and the illumination had come on, the windows were shuttered automatically by a cover that relaxed in the cool of the evening and slowly descended over the openings. Celene came back and made a delicious dinner of fish, fruits and salad for them and left again. Victor continued to inquire as to things that occurred to him as he put the idea of the spiritual world intersecting with our physical world together in his mind. Finally he fell silent and stared at them.

Jack felt the anointing of Yahveh heavy on himself and reached out and put his hand on Victor's shoulder. "Remember, our little minds cannot conceive of the things of Yahveh, His ways are higher than our ways, and His thoughts are higher than our thoughts. It is good to gain an understanding of the concepts because faith comes from hearing and hearing from the word of Yahveh. But, it is in your heart that you find Yahveh. Not in your thoughts and concepts. Too many people have a mind for Yahveh but their hearts are far away from Him. Do you mind if we pray together?"

Victor was still attempting to recover from the electricity that went through him when Jack had touched his shoulder. It had awoken something deep inside of him that was rising up to envelop him. He looked at Jack and said, "Do you really think Yahveh would want me to pray to Him? I mean, I have avoided Him for all these years and he probably isn't too thrilled with me."

Jack and Laura laughed quietly. Laura told Victor, "Don't humanize Yahveh. He isn't petty like people. He loves you and has waited your whole life to have a relationship with you. He probably has tears in His eyes right now, tears of happiness."

Victor smiled, "Now, who is humanizing Him?"

Jack reached out and took Laura's left hand in his right. They both reached over and took one of Victor's hands. Jack prayed. "Dear heavenly Father, we come humbled and with contrite hearts before your throne. We stand here and present Victor Chamberlain to you. Lord, he is a seeker of truth. You are truth. Touch him and talk to him Holy Spirit. Yahshua, show him the truth about Yourself and Your glory." Jack then began to pray quietly in his prayer language as did Laura. After a while they were all quiet. Jack opened his eyes to see the billionaire broken-hearted and crying quietly. Jack and Laura got up and sat on either side of him and prayed that the Lord would grant him peace and understanding, yes, even wisdom.

Sometime later Victor had composed himself and said, "I never knew. I never took time to seek Him out. He showed me just how much an idol I had made out of my money, my abilities, my fortune. I see now that He gave that all to me. I always thought I was the one that did it all. He showed me hundreds of times where what I did would have failed if He hadn't shown me the way quietly or arranged things so that my efforts succeeded. I was such an egotistic fool."

Jack patted his hand. "Welcome to the club. That is what I still have to battle today. But He makes it easier to see every day that I am His child and He is in charge."

Laura frowned, "I wish we had a Bible that wouldn't explode. I would like you to have it Victor so that you can read the word of Yahveh for yourself."

He sat there and stared at her. "Do you know, that is the first thing anybody has offered to give me out of the goodness of their heart since I got rich? Not looking for favor or return? I had forgotten what was like to be on the receiving end of a gift. Don't worry, I have a Bible around here somewhere and I will find it and read it. But I really want to reach out to Yahveh, to be closer to Him. I find a great peace in Him that has been missing my entire life." He sighed, a big sigh. "I think we have to do something to get rid of these murderers and let me get back in control of my estate."

Jack looked at Laura with concern. Victor saw the look, "Don't worry about that either. I just realized how much good my wealth could do for the world. I can honestly say that I have been happier here, penniless, than I had been for a long time with my billions. Now I realize I could do all sorts of things for Yahveh."

Jack held up his hand. "Victor, remember that all that wealth is Yahveh's, not yours, we are just stewards of His money. Also, it is great to want to do things for Yahveh, just don't let your "ministry" of works for Yahveh come between you and Him. Many preachers and Ministers fall into that trap of Satan's. They start out to glorify Yahveh and in the process they end up serving their own creation, whether it's a church, a foreign mission, whatever. The service becomes the idol and Yahveh is relegated to a secondary position. He doesn't like that. Also, you need to relax and realize that it is not through your strength, mind, will, or power, but through Yahveh's Holy Spirit that all things will be done. You need to ask Yahveh to help you decide what to do and when."

Victor's fast mind had listened and perceived in parallel to Jack's talk. It came as a revelation to him that he could find Yahveh one minute and then distance himself again in an effort to please Yahveh. There was a lot more he needed to learn about Yahveh. "How can I be saved?" He asked them.

Jack led him in the prayer of salvation where Victor admitted he was a sinner, that he believed that Christ had been raised from the dead and asked Christ to come into his heart, to be his Lord and Master, to be his very best friend. Victor found Yahshua waiting for him and also that he hadn't cried himself dry of tears.

He wanted to make his public confession of faith by being baptized and he didn't want to wait until the morning. Jack and Laura asked him of any way to contact the outside world and to warn their friends, Mark and Sarah, that they were being hunted. Jack showed Victor the watch/communicators they had been given and he thought that he might be able to provide a power source for them, tomorrow. He was too excited to do any research right then. He sat there for a few seconds and then said, "I'm fairly new at this, but I get the impression that we don't need to do anything to help your friends at this time. I believe that is what the Lord is placing in my spirit."

Victor then got up and went out to his neighbors and knocked on their doors and invited them to his baptism. He then went down to the pool they all swam in and waited for everyone to show up. When a sufficient crowd of his friends were there Jack and he got into the pool and Jack baptized him in the name of Yahshua.

Afterward he held an impromptu party and talked without tiring about his new friend. There was a great honesty in him that showed through whenever he talked about Yahshua and heaven. Whenever he got stuck for a lack of knowledge he turned to Jack or Laura. They did the best they could to answer everything that came up. The party ended around four a.m. Victor led them back to his house and deferred any discussion of what they were going to do tomorrow until later in the morning. He started to show them into a guest bedroom when Jack stopped him and earnestly asked him to consider doing something for their friends.

Victor stopped and saw that Jack and Laura were really concerned about the welfare of their friends. So he asked what they wanted him to do.

Jack thought for a minute and explained to the billionaire that Mark and Sarah would do almost anything to attempt to rescue them and were in grave danger regardless. They needed to get a message to the Israeli Mossad aircraft that would be going over at seven in the morning.

Victor thought about it and said that he would work on the communications later after sleep but that he would let the people of the island know about the possibility of Mark and Sarah trying to sneak onto the island. He looked at Jack and said, "I really don't think that they will be able to surmount the defenses I created for the seaward approaches."

Laura laughed and told him, "Mark is an ex-SEAL and a top counter-terrorism expert and his wife is recently of the Mossad. If they can't get on this island I would be highly surprised."

Re-estimating his original thoughts on the subject he nodded and went to the front door and rang a bell that hung on a hook outside the door. A man responded quickly to the summons even at that early hour. He spoke with Victor briefly and then left. Victor came back and showed them to their bedroom and bade them good night after hugging both of them and telling them that this was the best day of his life.

CHAPTER NINETEEN

As Jack and Laura fell into an exhausted sleep worrying about Mark and Sarah, the objects of their concern were less than four miles away from them and moving closer every minute.

The absolute black of the ocean bottom at five a.m. was clear to the infrared goggles and lights of the two scuba divers approaching the island. As the bottom shoaled rapidly upward, the twosome moved to a slow crawl. Objects in a regular pattern became clear in the infrared light. Stopping all forward motion the larger scuba diver slowly examined the objects and pushed a button on his wrist pack.

Mark's voice came clearly but softly to Sarah's left ear. "It's a full anti-invasion net. It runs from the floor to the water's surface, more or less. It is the latest version too. There's no way to fake it out, cut it, or get around it without setting off a dozen alarms."

Sarah considered the problem. Jack and Laura were being held captive on the island and they hadn't communicated since their abduction. Therefore there had to be a way to circumvent the security net to allow her and Mark onto the island without having to kill all the people, at least, not at first. "What do you think we should do? Can we tunnel under it?"

Mark examined the bottom anchors and replied, "No, the anchors are trembler sensors also. They'd pick up our activity within a few shovelfuls."

Mark checked the time left in their tanks, and started doing something he had never been taught in the service. He started praying, asking Yahveh for the solution to the problem. He knew he was good but he knew the Holy Spirit was a whole lot better.

While he was praying he noticed a movement to his right and he turned the infrared light on it. It was a medium-sized tiger shark. It was being drawn by their movement. Right now it was just curious. Then Mark realized what Yahveh was offering him. He reached into his satchel and withdrew a stun stick. Waiting until the shark was within range he reached out and shocked the shark. The charge wasn't fatal but did disable the shark for a short time. He called to Sarah, "Come on over here and help me issue our invitation to the party."

Sarah was somewhat disconcerted when she saw the three-hundred pound shark her husband was wrestling into a position facing the net. But she swam over and helped him move it close to the alarm net. Mark moved behind the shark and started pushing it towards the net as hard as he could swim. Sarah joined in and added to the momentum. The shark was recovering faster than Mark had hoped as they neared the net but only added to the force by trying to get away from the divers.

The shark hit the net hard enough to rip a dozen of the anchors out of the floor bed and collapse the net for a distance of ten to twelve feet. Mark and Sarah swam past the broken net and into the shallow water behind it. The shark recovered from the stun stick and found itself inside the net that had prevented it from reaching the schools of fish closer to the island. It had a field day in the shallows causing a tremendous splashing and thrashing of hundreds of fish trying to escape the predator in all directions.

Mark led Sarah to the north, away from the slaughter field and into a cove. Turning off his infrared lights he slowly raised his head above the surface and surveyed the beach and the edge of the tree line about twenty feet from the waterline. Slowly sliding back under the water he outlined the next challenge to his wife. "There are two video cameras covering this stretch of beach. Doubtless there are trip wires or trembler switches, or possibly an IR fence inside the tree line to detect people trying to avoid the cameras. How do we handle this one, Spy Lady?"

Sarah had also turned off her infrared lamp and she repeated Mark's surveillance of the shoreline. "We can time out the sweeps of the two cameras and one of us can watch for IR stuff with our goggles. The other should go to night-vision goggles to look for temblors, wires, and possibly Claymore mines."

Mark agreed and they made their preparations while watching the sweeps of the cameras. At the right moment, Mark slid out of the water and wiggled to a large boulder in the sand. Several minutes later, when the cameras were not covering his area for a few seconds he rose to a crouch and dashed to the tree line. He tried to become part of a bush as the views of the cameras returned. Checking carefully with his night-vision goggles he moved outside the camera's coverage area. Sarah moved up next to him after timing out the cameras in the cycle behind Mark. She used her IR goggles but didn't see any visible IR. She switched to the other IR frequencies but didn't find anything. Mark started to move inland slowly, watching for booby-traps and other sensors like additional cameras.

After they had traveled three hundred feet they found a large bush with sufficient coverage to hide them from the morning's light and having carefully erased their tracks they settled down to wait for full light before making their next move.

CHAPTER TWENTY

Mark attempted to analyze his emotions as he watched his wife sleep. He had never thought that he would love anybody as much as he did Sarah. Of course, there were times in his background he might of gotten killed and not of come back to meet her. Before he fell in love with her he hadn't really worried about if he would come back or not. Now he realized that what he did affected her too. He thought back to another island invasion he had been part of as the leader of a U.S. Navy SEAL team.

------------------------******-----------------------

There hadn't been any electronic fences or trembler sensors to block the way in for his eight-man force. They had reached the island's shore without incident and had transitioned over the beach into the jungle without any problems. They had submerged the two-man tow-engines that had brought them there from the submarine and covered them with sand and debris so that they couldn't be detected from the air. They had also erased any sign that eight men had crossed the beach into the tree line. So far, so good!

As he studied the map he checked the GPS coordinates and communicated with his commander via satellite. The stolen missiles should be only about two miles from his present position. An hour there, four to find and destroy the missiles, an hour back and they should be headed back to the submarine by lunch time.

He broke the team into two, four-man squads and proceeded to the target area. The jungle was noisy around them as they ghosted forward, watching for sentries and booby-traps along the way. The sun rose in the sky and the humidity became intense. The sweat was dripping down his back as Mark reached the target area. After fifty minutes of searching and careful recon Mark was upset. There were no missiles there. There was nothing there. There wasn't any sign that another human being had ever walked in that part of the world. He sent the troops the opposite direction for a second search, nothing.

Calling on the satellite phone he reported the situation to his control. Instead of telling him to pack it in and head back to the sub they told him to wait for orders. So, he waited, and waited, and waited.

Four hours later, when he had just about decided that the satellite had fallen out of the sky they got a message. "Papa Joe to bad boy the tour is exactly at your coordinates. The GPS position of the missiles is now confirmed by two successive satellite passes over your area. Find the target and eliminate it, end."

Mark called the team together and explained the delay and the problem. "We're here and the satellites say the missiles are here but we know that they are not here. That leads to one of two conclusions. One, the Intel and the satellite data is wrong, or two, we're not looking in the right places."

Mark's second in command, Lt. John Crowley asked, "Where should we be looking then?"

Mark gestured in a wide arc with his arm. "We've looked over every inch of this part of the island and found nothing, not even a human footprint." He looked up into the sky. "The missiles are not up there." He looked at the ground under his feet. "So that only leaves one dimension, down."

Looking around he spotted a tall tree that had grown above the rest of the jungle. He sent their best climber to climb the tree and look down on the local area. After the man came back down he reported the only anomaly in the surface area that he could see was a rise in the land with a large pile of rocks on top of it. The squad quick-timed it over to the rocks and investigated them. Mark was first to spot the hole. It was actually on the upper side of one of the huge rocks. Climbing up onto the rock he looked down the crevice. It wasn't man made but he could feel a warm wet draft of air coming up the crevice.

Mark and John dropped their packs and worked their way into the crevice and downward. About fifteen feet down the crevice began to widen out and they had to stop because there were no more hand holds to hang onto. Climbing back up, Mark took one of the coils of rope they had and fixed it to his web harness. Arranging the proper signals with the other men he had them lower him down into the crevice. After it widened out he dropped another twenty feet and signaled them to stop lowering him. He could see a dim light below him and also that the crevice widened out even more.

Mark slowly rotated on the rope until his head was down and his feet were up. He signaled for a slow descent. As he dropped he kept close watch for any form of surveillance. He suddenly signaled stop and his descent halted. His head was only partially below a ledge in the edge of the crevice but what he could see startled him. He carefully noted everything he could and then signaled to be pulled back up. After he reached the top and was out of the crevice he motioned the men to come away from the crevice for a conference.

Mark took a small notebook out of his pack and drew on it. "The crevice opens up into a natural cave. The cave obviously has an underwater inlet from the sea. They've built a dock arrangement down there and there are two full sized submarines docked there. They are side by side with about twenty feet between them. There are areas for maintenance and recreation and there's at least sixty men moving around down there. Across the cave to the right I saw the Super Sparrow Missile crates. Whether or not the missiles are in there I don't know but we have to find out."

John asked, "With that many enemies how are we going to do that?

Mark smiled, "We'll wait until 1 a.m. and sneak pass them. I figure the majority will be asleep at that time."

He explained how he wanted to run the op. "Three men need to stay up here to lower the other five down one at a time. Once down, three of you will cover John and me as we try to determine if the missiles are actually in the crates. If they are, we'll set some charges and try to make it back here to the crevice. If we're undetected at that point we'll extract one at a time and blow the birds after we're all out."

Mark knew there were a ton of unknowns in his plan but they didn't know when the missiles might be moved again and therefore they had to move tonight. He used the sat-phone to relay all the information to his controller and ask for specific backup aid.

Everybody tried to get as much rest as possible as darkness fell over the island. Mark's wrist alarm woke him at 0000 hours. He checked with the guard and started making preparations. He packed four C-4 packages with timed and radio detonators and added an extra Cold Steel Tanto knife to his outfit. He took four fragmentation grenades and his silenced pistol. Using combat cosmetics he darkened his face and hands. At 0045 hours he was ready

Their roles designated and rehearsed, the team worked quietly and efficiently, lowering the five men to the floor of the cave. With their darkened skin and dark uniforms they blended into the rocks of the cave wall. The three man support team took their positions and waited.

Mark and John moved closer to the area of the submarines. They could see the two guards walking beats on either side of the boats. Obviously the guards had done this hundreds of times before and had never had any problems. They were used to seeing nothing unusual and the two SEALs tried to keep it that way. Whenever a guard was walking towards them they froze and didn't move until the unsuspecting sentry had turned away again.

They took almost twenty agonizing minutes to cross the distance to the far wall and move past the sleeping men in the barracks room. It took ten more minutes to go down past the kitchen area and get behind the missile crates.

Once there, Mark kept watch while John silently cut an access port in the side of one crate. Quietly moving the cut out piece of crate aside, John reached into the hole with a mini-mag flash light and let out the smallest beam of light between his fingers he could. He was staring at a Super Sparrow nuclear-tipped anti-ship missile. He turned out the light and replaced the panel carefully. When he was done it would take a close inspection to see the intrusion.

John tugged on Mark's pants leg. When Mark knelt down John confirmed the presence of the missiles. Mark took two of the charges out of his pack and put both detonators into the Plastique. He set the timer detonator for one hour. He set both of the radio detonators to the same frequency.

Mark removed John's cut panel and placed one of the charges directly onto the fuel section of the missile. The magnets that held the charge in place were stronger than he expected and the charge snapped to the missile with a definite "thump". Both of the men froze and looked between the missile crates at the nearest sentry.

The man had stopped and looked in their direction. He stood there for a while and then resumed his patrol. Apparently strange noises happened in the cave every now and then.

John looked at Mark and made a gesture like wiping his brow in relief. Mark smiled and replaced the cut out panel again. He took the second charge and placed it on the floor under the bottom crate. He pushed it out of sight.

As they were getting ready to retreat to the crevice Mark stopped John. He held up the other two charges and pointed at the submarines. John's eyes opened wide and he made the universal signal of insanity by rotating his finger near the side of his head.

Mark told John to head back to the crevice and he moved to the end of the crates to await his chance to sneak over to the first submarine. John stopped him and took one of the charges from him. He then smiled and pointed at the far sub and then at Mark. Mark nodded and watched the closer guard. When the man was most of the way to the far end of the walkway next to the closest sub, Mark slid out from behind the crates and silently snuck over to the submarine. He lowered himself down to the hull of the sub as the guard made his turn.

The next time the guard was close to the far end, John duplicated Mark's run and joined him under the walkway. One more time the guard marched his beat and Mark slid into the water and submerged. Swimming under water he reached the other sub and pushed himself down to the bottom of the curve in the hull. This was where the outer and inner hulls were the closest together. He carefully attached this one and set the timers. He then slowly came to the surface to see that John had done the same.

They carefully swam to the end of the sub pen closest to their exit and waited until the guards would go to the far ends of the sub pen. Unfortunately the two men weren't walking the same beats. One man was coming back while the other was walking away. The two SEALs looked at each other. Mark carefully drew his silenced pistol from its holster.

Suddenly the guard farthest away turned and hurried towards them. Mark knew he and John were close to invisible in the dark under the walkway but he was about to take the shot when John's hand on his arm stopped him.

With a pounding of feet, three more soldiers came to a halt directly above the two SEALs. The first two sentries hurried up to the threesome and stopped. Everyone saluted each other and the first two guards marched away with the third man while the other two men started patrolling the sub pen. John leaned over to Mark and whispered in his ear, "Great! Shift change. These new guys will be a lot sharper for a while."

Mark looked at his watch. Thirty minutes had gone by since he had set the one-hour timers. He whispered back to John, "We don't have a while!" and pointed at his watch. John nodded.

The two new sentries did give the SEALs a break. They were walking their beats in unison. As they walked away from the nose of the submarines, John and Mark climbed carefully up to the walkway and rolled across it to the other side. They slid behind some crates and waited for the guards to make their next march away from them. John pointed to the wet place where they had left the water but there was nothing that could be done about the trail.

Fortunately the sentries didn't come to the middle of the walkway but just walked their beats back and forth alongside the submarines. Timing it out, the two SEALs made it back to the three man covering team in less than fifteen minutes. Mark told them, "We've got less than ten minutes to get back up and start moving away from this area."

The men nodded and the first one tied on the rope and signaled for a rapid ascent. He rose quickly and quietly. The procedure was repeated four more times until Mark climbed out of the crevice and they all took off in the direction of the beach where they had landed. After they had gone about three kilometers, Mark stopped them and pulled out the trigger box. He extended the antenna and pushed the red buttons numbered three and four. Two distinct "thumps" were felt where the SEALs stood. Mark looked at John, "No more submarines." He then pushed the red buttons numbered one and two. This time there was substantially more violence. The whole island shook and a huge section of the jungle flew up into the air followed by giant gouts of fire and debris. The exploding of the missiles knocked all eight of the SEALs to the ground and pelted them with rocks and clods of dirt.

Not knowing if additional explosions would occur they got up and ran for the beach. Reaching the beach they found their wet suits where they had hidden them. Putting them on in short order, the eight SEALs waded into the surf and dived into the water. Swimming several hundred feet away from the beach they dived to the bottom and retrieved their power units.

As they were getting ready to head back to their submarine they were buffeted around in the water as a large body passed close to them. Mark looked up to see the hull of a submarine no more than fifty feet away.

The SEALs watched as the boat slowed and started to surface. Mark clicked on his underwater infrared communicator and called John. "What type of boat is that?"

John aligned his transmitter towards Mark, "It looks like a Russian hunter/ killer sub."

Mark asked, "Is it friend or a foe?"

John returned, "Your guess is as good as mine."

Mark thought for a second, "If it is unfriendly then our sub won't stand a chance against this."

John shot back, "Yeah, but if it's friendly we really shouldn't sink it."

Mark smiled to himself, "True, but that doesn't mean we can't play with it."

Mark pulled his pack off of the sled and took out two more C-4 charges. He quickly put radio detonators in them and swam towards the Russian submarine. It was still surfacing so his noises would be lost in the general noise of the operation. The rest of the SEALs continued to swim under the sub and head out to sea.

Mark swam to the rear of the sub and then up to the huge bronze propellers. The Russian sub had two props on separate shafts, one inside the other so that the props were aligned one in front of the other. Mark took a calculated risk that the props wouldn't start again and reached between them and fastened one of the charges to a single blade on the forward prop. He repeated the operation on a single blade of the rearward prop. He then swam strongly to catch up with the other SEALs.

When they were two hundred feet away from the Russian sub he detonated the charges. The water transmitted the dual "thumps" clearly to the SEALs. They turned on their sleds and were towed out into deeper water.

Finding their submarine where it was supposed to be Mark placed a hydrophone against the hull and spoke to the watch commander. "Sir, we are back but do not surface."

The answer came back quickly, "Why not, Captain?"

Mark raised his eyebrows, a motion lost to anyone else not inside his mask. "Because there is a Russian Hunter/Killer sub three thousand yards off your starboard bow."

"Okay Captain, use the Emergency Hatch."

Two by two the seals tied down their sleds and entered the emergency hatch to be cycled into the submarine. Mark and John were the last to enter. After shedding his wet suit and drying off, Mark went up and met with the XO on the sub's bridge. "Did you get a make on that Russian sub, Sir?"

The Executive Officer nodded, "It's the Romanov, an Alpha class and a nasty competitor. It's a good thing we're not on opposite sides this time."

Mark swallowed quickly, "What does that mean Sir?"

The XO looked at the SEAL Captain, "It means that we aren't enemies right now. They are here to investigate a stolen submarine or something."

John had walked in and listened to the last several exchanges. He covered his eyes with his hand. "Oh... Boy!"

The XO frowned and looked at Mark, "Why is your number two saying Oh boy?"

Mark tried to think of a way to put a good spin on what had happened but couldn't come up with one. "Well Sir, we didn't know if they were friendly or not so we handicapped them so that they wouldn't be able to mess with you or something like that."

The XO's frown deepened, "Okay Captain, tell me how you "handicapped" a non-belligerent submarine." Several in the crew were all ears at this point. John was trying to blend into the background any way he could.

Mark smiled, "Well Sir, you know how those Alphas have two, ten-bladed props?" When the XO nodded, Mark continued. "Well I arranged for them to only have two, nine-bladed props instead." Mark then waited for the explosion.

The XO's eyes had grown wider when Mark explained what he had done. For several seconds he just stood there. Then he erupted in laughter. "Son, you have belled the cat! That Alpha is going to sound like a tramp steamer and shake and vibrate all the way back to Mother Russia for repairs. This I have to tell the Captain about." He was still laughing as he made his way aft, "Bosn's Mate Albert, you have the Conn," floated back from the XO.

Mark was suddenly the hero of the hour. All the ratings on the sub wanted to shake his hand. He was happy to oblige but didn't understand why until sometime later when one of the crew clued him in.

The diving plane rating was still laughing as he shook Mark's hand. Seeing the look of confusion on Mark's face, he pulled the SEAL to the side and explained the reaction of the XO and the crew. "You really have to be a submariner to appreciate what you did, apparently by accident. The big contest under the water is between our Los Angeles class attack subs and the Russian Alphas. It's like a struggle between two excellent quarterbacks on the same football team. Both want to be the best. But, there can only be one "best". Anything that can embarrass an Alpha is considered wonderful on our submarines and what you did is probably the most embarrassing thing that could happen to them. It is obvious to them that you could have sunk them, but no, you spiked their props instead. The missing blades will cause them to vibrate like mad, reduce their speed under water or on the surface, and set up a racket that can be heard for miles under the sea.

See, it's like having to run to the pits in a NASCAR race with a flat tire! While everybody else roars by you and thumbs their nose at you! You have no idea how deflating your little "handicapping" is to the Alpha submariners. This will be talked about for years. Not only that, but we were here to witness it. They can't claim mechanical failure and limp home with their noses in the air because an American sub was close by. Wonderful." With that the rating walked off and left Mark feeling grateful for anything.

Later the XO was taking the SEALs action reports and commented to Mark, "You know if you had sunk them it would have been a black eye for the Navy and your file would have gotten lost somewhere. It was a good choice you made. I understand the wags are now calling the Romanov, the "gimp".

-----------------------*****-----------------------

As he returned his thoughts to the present, Mark shook his head in the bush next to Sarah and realized that Yahveh had been watching over him then, too.

CHAPTER TWENTY-ONE

After resting for several hours and watching the sun rise in the east, Mark pointed out a direction and they carefully slid out of the shrub and started moving slowly from cover to cover.

Mark was about to make another move when he became aware of a presence. He looked slowly around and discovered a short, brown man standing near a tree about ten feet from him. The man was relaxed and staring directly at him. He was dressed in a short covering on his waist and had nothing in the way of weapons. So, since he was already detected, Mark got up without looking at Sarah who slowly pivoted and covered Mark with a silenced pistol. Mark knew she could drive nails with that gun and he wasn't worried about her professionalism. So he slowly walked over to the man.

Approaching the smaller man, Mark was surprised when he smiled and spoke to him by name, "Mr. Connelly? If you and your, well-armed wife, will accompany me, the Gardener is expecting you as soon as possible."

Mark shook his head. "Well, I guess all the sneaking in wasn't worth the effort was it?"

The man smiled again, "The Gardener didn't think you two would actually make it this far without setting off the evil men's alarms. I, for one, am quite surprised that I saw you at all. You're really quite good at this aren't you?"

Mark motioned Sarah to join them and started following the smaller man. "May I ask your name and that of the Gardener?"

"My name is probably unpronounceable to you but you may call me Oliver. I learned my English at Harvard and Yale in your country. The Gardener's name I will let him tell you. He and his guests were quiet worried about you and will be eager to see you. So please hurry along."

Shaking his head again Mark made eye contact with Sarah that said, "Be careful, I don't know if I trust this guy or not." Sarah nodded and followed them both as they approached a large rock.

Twenty minutes later they were being led up the stairs to a quaint little cottage in the jungle. After several knocks the door was opened by a tall black man who greeted them both with a hug. Mark could have chuckled at the scene. The black man wore a casual shirt and slacks, Oliver had his one-piece outfit and somewhat looming over them were Mark and Sarah in black suits, armed to the teeth and outweighing the others by a good hundred pounds.

They were shown into a comfortable setting room while the black man excused himself for a few minutes. About five minutes later Jack and Laura came around the corner and grabbed the armed couple in bear hugs.

Jack slapped Mark on the back and said, "It's good to see you're still alive."

Everyone laughed and Mark and Sarah relaxed. "Well", said Sarah, "It took some real daring-do to get here to rescue you, but it looks like you don't need rescuing."

Laura shook her head, "You couldn't be more wrong. We have a lot to talk about. First, tell us how you got here so quick."

Mark set his silenced sub-machine gun on the side table and looked seriously at the Malones. "We had to get here quickly because things on this island are much worse than we thought."

CHAPTER TWENTY-TWO

Jack and Laura gave Mark and Sarah a while to get settled and relax and then they met with Victor in his combination meeting room and office.

Jack related how they had come to be at Victor's and the state of the situation as far as they could tell. Victor's infiltration of the communication net at his mansion and the video coverage across the island was a real advantage but the lack of off-island communications was a serious hang-up that Jack hoped Mark would be able to resolve for them.

Mark and Sarah listened to the story from that end and then told their side.

Mark smiled as he recalled the parting at the airport. "You know we had a chance of beating those goons with the submachine guns don't you? Still, I think you did the right thing to let them take us home while you went on to the island."

Jack nodded and added, "But I still don't understand how you got back from the States so quickly."

Sarah frowned, "We never went to America. They had planned to kill us once we were asleep and dump our bodies into the ocean. It was an obvious ploy. We suckered them into thinking we were soundly asleep when all there was in the beds were pillow people. Two of them came in with silenced pistols and "killed" the pillow people. We reciprocated. Then the pilot and copilot decided to become stupid and try to take us. All four of them are resting in the deep somewhere about six hours from here. Mark was able to fly us to the NATO airbase in Australia and we were able to get some SEAL team assistance and equipment. Ten hours later we were back here."

Mark explained how they circumnavigated Victor's defenses and then how they met Oliver and came to be in the room with the people they came to rescue.

Then Sarah became even more serious. Her face showed the concern she was feeling. The little lines around her eyes and mouth became more pronounced as her eyes narrowed and, if looks could kill, someone would be dead right then. "While we were at the NATO base I contacted the Mossad and the new information they gave me isn't good." She looked at each of the others to see that she had their undivided attention. "Kareem Kalifah is on this island. Seems he has been here for four years. He ran the operations against Israel and the U.S. from here. Worse yet, a Russian nuclear scientist was caught by the unnamed sources and turned over to the Mossad. He was attempting to leave the Middle East with falsified papers. It seems he had been aiding the Iranian government and he provided some distressing news as a way to lessen his punishment. It has been confirmed that over the last four years Victor's money has purchased the necessary equipment and raw materials for producing a thermonuclear weapon. All of this equipment was transshipped back and forth to conceal its destination. The captured scientist was here until last year when his part of the project was completed. They had a plant producing weapons grade nuclear material in November of last year."

Jack interrupted her, "I assume that the bomb he is building will be used against Israel."

She nodded, "Oh yeah, according to the scientist he has a "Chamberlain Food Services" vehicle that is designed to carry the bomb into Jerusalem without it being detected. Since it is a good-will gesture on the behalf of Victor Chamberlain to the poor people of Jerusalem it will be welcomed."

Laura was horrified, "But, if the Mossad know about it can't they stop it?"

"There is a lot of friction between the Israelis and the Arabs living in Jerusalem and they have to have in-controversial proof of the bomb's existence before they can accuse the Chamberlain people or there will be riots beyond any we've seen so far as the Arabs cry out against the Jews for denying free food for the poor in Jerusalem. Most of the poor are Arab you see. Plus there will be forty identical trucks making the trip from three different directions. The Mossad have no idea which truck this super-hidden package of death is in. They can't stop them all on the word of a criminal without the world rushing to war in anger."

Jack shook his head, "The sad part is that at least half of the people killed will be non-Jews. They don't have any idea of how their anger is being used to kill them and make a major terroristic statement."

Sarah continued, "You can be sure that the preparation is in place to blame Israel for the explosion and deaths too. This cannot be allowed to happen."

Victor Chamberlain looked at Sarah. "I'm truly sorry that these fiends are using my organization to do this horrible thing. But, I have a question." His brilliant mind hadn't been dulled by being in the forest for six years. "Are you sure that this Kareem told the scientist the truth? I ask that because I am fairly certain that they have been building a rocket launch site on the other side of the island. They would have to launch across India and Saudi Arabia but I don't think they would care about air space violations."

Mark asked, "Do you think they have a rocket?"

Victor put his hands up in the universal gesture of inability to answer. "I really don't know if they do or not. I have no links into that part of the operation and they don't discuss it on the channels I can intercept."

Jack had been thinking about what he knew and the new information that Mark had provided. "Victor, I think they know you listen into them. Remember that they instructed their people to get rid of Mark and Sarah on the plane. Yet when we listened to them discussing our deaths they said that kidnapping them was the next step. That doesn't make any sense unless they knew you were listening in and they were playing to confuse you."

Victor asked, "Do you think they really think you are dead?"

Jack thought about that for a second, "I really don't know if they're sure we're dead or not."

Sarah slapped her hand on the table. "It doesn't really matter what they think! If you are correct then we need to find that missile base and stop them from launching against Israel. I agree that the truck thing is a ruse because they let the scientist leave knowing that he would talk if captured. These are some very smart cookies. They win if Israel stops the trucks because there will be no bomb found. Yet they can still strike from the air and probably blame it on someone else. Victor, can you show us on a map where the base is?"

Victor smiled, "Yes, but I can do better than that. I will take you there." His attitude did not allow any argument about his safety. He had found Yahshua and he wasn't worried about his future anymore. He was going to do the right thing.

CHAPTER TWENTY-THREE

Planning their raid took most of the day to find out everything the villagers knew about the base and piecing it together. Late that afternoon, after Mark and Sarah shared their weapons with the others, the five set off for the secret base on the other side of the island. Using Victor's underground cart system they moved to within two miles of the site. They exited the system and started moving on foot.

Mark and Sarah led as they were the most experienced at this kind of fieldcraft. When they came to the first defenses they stopped and Laura suggested that they pray for success. After the heartfelt prayer, considering the odds, they moved past the defenses and approached the actual site. Sarah pointed out the probable building housing a missile and they approached it in the evening dimness.

Mark surveyed the entrances and found them both alarmed and heavily guarded by at least four guards. Sliding back to the group as night fell, he summed the situation up. "We can either eliminate the guards at one of the entrances and set off the alarms and try to get past the automatic defenses that will be set off, or, we can try to find a stealthier way in, which will take more time."

Victor asked, "What is the rush, don't we have time?"

Mark and Sarah both shook their heads. Sarah answered him. "See the white vapor coming out of those exhaust stacks? That means that the missile has been fueled for launch. They don't do that until they are ready to fire the missile. I don't know that we have any time at all."

The urgency of the situation became clear to everyone. Jack thought for a few minutes and asked Mark, "Would there be any chance we can get into the building where the pipes that bring the fuel go into the place?"

Mark and Sarah exchanged looks. Sarah said, "Might be a chance if they weren't too choosy on how they built it. Let's go look."

Careful of alarms and sensors the five people made a slow circuit of the building until they could see a small access door next to the incoming pipelines. Mark moved up to the door, checked for alarms, overcame the two that he found, and quickly overcame the locking mechanism. He waved the rest of the team up to the door. Looking in the now open door showed a three-foot high crawl space that led into the building. One by one they crawled into the dim light and looked at the engine of destruction standing there.

Mark swore quietly under his breath. When everyone looked at him quizzically, he explained. "That is a U.S. Air Force LGM-118 Peacekeeper ICBM. They were phased out in 1993 under an arms treaty with the Russians. This is a prototype of a specific modification designed to be independently targeted through the use of a special MIRV seeker head."

Sarah asked, "Wasn't the Peacekeeper a solid fuel rocket? Then why are there fuel lines?"

Mark smiled, "The Peacekeeper was a four-stage intercontinental ballistic missile with three solid fuel stages and a special fourth, liquid-fueled stage.

"It has a velocity of 15,000 m.p.h. with a ceiling of 500 miles and a range of over 6,800 miles. Its first stage was a Thiokol solid-fuel rocket with 500,000 pounds of thrust. The second stage was an Aerojet solid-fuel rocket and the third stage was a Hercules solid-fuel rocket that was designed to reach apogee. The fourth stage was used after the solid fuel rockets had gotten it into flight. It was designed for post-boost maneuvers and was powered by a Rocketdyne restartable liquid-fuel rocket, hence the fuel lines. Originally the warhead was a10x W-87-0 thermonuclear weapon with maximum of 300 kilotons formed in a 10x Mk.21 MIRV. It would have been able to hit ten different targets simultaneously. But, the warheads had been removed and destroyed in the early 1990s."

Laura spoke up, "That's why they had to spend four years developing their own bomb! They somehow got hold of the missile but had to buy or steal the technology to make a warhead."

Victor looked at the seventy-one foot tall missile with apprehension. "How do we go about stopping it?"

Mark shrugged, this was his specialty. "We blow up the missile, the control system, or we bag everyone here and take control of it."

Victor shook his head, "You can't blow it up if there is any chance the warhead could go off. There are at least three hundred innocent people on the island and they would all be killed."

Jack nodded, "He's got a good point. We need to find some other way to prevent the launch or the strike."

Mark sighed, "Okay, I actually studied the guidance system for this missile in my early years in the service. Let me see if I can't jimmy the system on the missile or find a way to shut it down completely. You four see if you can find the control room and prevent anybody from pushing the button while I'm inside working on the missile."

The two men and two women moved out to look for a way into the control room while Mark scaled the service gantry up to the top of the missile.

Reaching the access panel to the guidance system, Mark took out a uni-tool from his pack and quickly unfastened and opened the panel. Sorting out the wiring and circuit boards of the fifteen-year old design he noticed some new things and stopped to study them for a bit. Smiling, he quickly moved a metal jumper and cut two other wires. Finishing his work he replaced the panel and cat walked across the beam of the gantry to the access door in the side of the launch cradle. Moving cautiously he moved in the direction he was sure the control room was located.

Hearing excited voices in Arabic and English he carefully opened the door in front of him and risked a quick look. It was a Mexican standoff between his team and four security guards who had taken a position behind the consoles and aimed their rifles at the team. Laura and Sarah were protected by door frames while Jack and Victor were behind some large computer bays. No one wanted to start shooting because it would damage the equipment not to mention the half-dozen technicians and scientists caught between the forces.

Mark had the angle on the security guards and aimed his Mac-11 at them. "Put your weapons down, NOW!" he yelled. The guards, realizing they were in a crossfire position, decided to comply rather than die. They put their weapons on the floor and raised their hands. The team quickly removed any other weapons they had, tied their hands behind them, and locked them inside a storeroom.

Sarah collared the most important looking person running the equipment and interrogated him on the spot. He admitted that they were about to launch the missile at Israel whenever Kareem told them to. They had noticed the intrusion committed by Mark by an open access panel light but had not had time to report it because the rest of the team had commanded their attention for the last few minutes. Mark asked, "Where is Kareem?"

The scientist answered, "He's at the mansion but I think he's on his way here for the actual launch." The scientist was distracted by activity on the video panel at his desk. "In fact, he's coming up in the elevator right now."

Mark ordered everyone back to their positions and warned them not to give Kareem any indication that they were there if they didn't want to quit breathing.

The team hid behind panels and waited until the terrorist and his two bodyguards walked into the control room. They were celebrating their arrival to announce the launch with much glee. To say that they were shocked by the appearance of the team would have been a large understatement. Jack and Mark quickly disarmed them and bound the bodyguards. They then took them to the storeroom and added them to the guards already there.

Sarah watched the fanatical light behind Kareem's eyes as he prayed, thought, and tried to find a way to reverse their situation. He glanced at the panels on the consoles in front of the technicians. Sarah knew he was about to do something foolish and she kept her Sig-Sauer 9MM's silencer pointed directly at the man.

Suddenly Kareem seemed to faint. He staggered and fell towards the console. He screamed in victory as he smashed the final button to launch the missile. He also died at the same time with a bullet to the head.

The building started vibrating like a 7.0 earthquake was happening. Then a giant roar came from the launch building and with an explosion so loud it partially deafened everyone in the building, the roof flew off and the Peacemaker lifted into sight with a light to rival the sun behind it. It gathered speed and roared up through the night sky in a definite arc to the west.

Sarah turned to her husband with worry in her heart but it faded away as she saw the smile on his face.

All at once armed guards were at all the entrances with their rifles pointed at the team members. As the odds climbed from five to one towards ten or more to one, Mark dropped his sub gun to the floor and raised his hands. Taking a cue from him the rest of the team followed suit and were soon bound up and being escorted down to the first floor.

CHAPTER TWENTY-FOUR

Forced to their knees on the reception room floor, the five team members kept their silence. The guards were very wary and also did not talk. After ten minutes the front doors opened to a group of men who walked over to the group and stood there appraising the commandos.

One man who seemed to be the leader stepped forward and grabbed Laura by the jaw and pulled her head upward so that he could look at her face. Jack tensed himself but a rifle barrel pressed against his neck and he held himself in check. The man repeated the operation with each of the others until he was finished. He stepped back and nodded his head. "I think we have the group we want. Take them to the reactor building."

The guards jerked them to their feet and moved them along outside and over a long path to a concrete building with the round dome shape of a nuclear plant. When they stopped outside the building the leader had them lined up side by side. He gestured to five of the six men with him. "You don't need to know these men's names." He pointed at the bullet-headed man. "Ivan, the Malones we have already met. I am Hiram Lallatun. We comprise the operating group that runs Mr. Chamberlain's company." He looked at Victor. "Isn't that so, Mr. Chamberlain?" He walked over to the tall black man and spoke softly to him. "You broke the rules Victor. You weren't supposed to cause trouble. That is too bad for you."

The wind coming across the island was a pleasant evening breeze, with smells of the jungle plants behind the nuclear dome. The sky was dark with hundreds of stars. It was a seemingly unconcerned universe that watched the little pageant taking place on the island.

Hiram turned to Jack. "Okay, Mr. Malone. Here is how things are going to happen. You are going to tell us where the crucifixion nail is and offer to take us to it right now or I will be forced to deal with you and your companions most severely."

Jack was four inches taller than Lallatun and his eyes were icy green at the moment. "As I told your lackey, Ivan, I have no interest in providing Yahveh's things to Satan's agents. Or, in language an uncultured snob like you can understand, No way."

Anger and irritation turned Lallatun's face into a mask of fury. "Fine, we'll get it another way. You have just chosen death for you and your companions." He started to walk off when Mark let out a big sigh. "Good! There for a minute I thought he was planning to talk us to death." When that resulted in smiles Lallatun wheeled around and smiled his own evil smile. "No, Mr. Connelly, your death is going to be far more gruesome than that. You, your friend Mr. Malone, and this pathetic loser of a billionaire are going to be given a five minute tour of our reactor core. In less than twenty minutes after that, your hair will fall out, followed quickly by your teeth and eyes. Giant sores will form on all your internal organs as well as your skin. In five more minutes you will be dead. I'm just sorry that your mind will go before your hair."

Laura spoke up. "I want to stay with my husband."

Lallatun smiled an even more evil smile. "No my dear, you and your Jewish playmate are going to have the opportunity to convince us to let you live. All of us." His implication was clear and since they were going to die anyway both Jack and Mark started for him but were both clubbed to the ground by rifle butts. Jack shook off the beating and stood up. He felt the Holy Spirit speak for him. "Lallatun, by commanding our deaths in this manner, you have just selected how Yahveh will destroy you and your group."

Lallatun shrugged, "Delude yourself with all the dreams you want to. I don't believe in your God. Anyway, I am more powerful than any god as Israel has just found out! Your threats are groundless and stupid. Go die."

The guards then dragged the two men to the reactor core airlock and threw them into it. Victor stepped in behind them and the massive door was closed and latched.

Mark rolled around and managed to bring his hands under his bottom and feet and get them in front of him. It only took him a few seconds to rub through a piece of the rope on a cross member inside the airlock. He then untied both Victor and Jack.

Victor looked at them both and said, "I've enjoyed knowing you both and I am sorry that we've so quickly come to such a miserable end."

Jack smiled and Mark just grunted. Jack put his hand on Victor's shoulder, "Don't give up yet. You are just a baby Christian but you are saved and your Yahveh is a lot bigger than this situation. Let's pray."

As they prayed to a loving Elohim to protect them and their wives and their newest member of the Church, Jack felt the anointing of the Holy Spirit fall more heavily than he could ever remember before. As they continued to praise the Lord and extol the majesty of Yahveh their hearts leaped and sang within them. Jack realized he was singing in tongues and that surprised him since he had never done it before.

The guards watching them through the closed circuit television shook their heads in wonderment of three men about to die a hideous death who could still raise their voices to their God. A lot of good that would do them in the radioactive hell they were about to enter. Just then Ivan stepped into the control room and told them to proceed with the executions. He started a video tape to record everything. He then used a microphone to speak to the three men in the airlock. "I see that you have made peace with your God but it is still not too late to give me what I want."

Jack replied, assuming that the sadistic security chief could hear him. He quoted from the Bible's book of David.

"Ivan, If we are thrown into the blazing furnace, the Elohim we serve is able to save us from it, and he will rescue us from your hand, but even if he does not, we want you and your minions to know, O Satan, that we will not serve you or provide that which you desire the most."

That made Ivan furious with them. He ordered the gates to the core opened to their maximum which was seven times more deadly than usual The three men, wearing their shirts, trousers, and other clothes, stood in the airlock as the inner door opened to a green hellish light. Then these three men, freely walked into the blazing room facing the open nuclear core.

Then Ivan leaped to his feet in amazement and asked his guards "Weren't there three men that we tied up and threw into the airlock?"

They all replied, "Yes sir."

Ivan said, "Look! I see four men standing and singing in the core room, unbound and unharmed, and the fourth looks like a man of light!"

Jack, Mark, and Victor were completely absorbed in their praise and worship of the Lord and the thought went haphazardly through the back of Jack's mind, "Where two or more of you gather in my name, there I will be also." He could sense the presence of the Lord Yahshua and his spirit sang in great joy. He had never known such bliss. His heart longed to share this with Laura.

Victor was so beyond words he couldn't imagine saying anything. He also felt the presence of the Lord and was transported to a marvelous place of peace, harmony, and contentment that soothed all the days and hurts from all his previous years. He would have stayed there forever if he could. His money, his power, his inventions were as meaningless as the mist.

Mark was equally in adoration but his spirit cried out for Sarah. How he wished she were with him and not in harm's way. He felt the Lord's hand touch him and all the worry left him as if it had never been. Mark knew his love was in Yahveh's hands and she would be safe."

Ivan looked back and forth between the monitor showing the video tape, which showed the three men, and the live monitor that showed four. He was interrupted by one of the guards, "Sir, those three guys have been in there for eight minutes already. They should be deader than stone by now!"

Ivan couldn't make sense of this. Then a light dawned in his mind. He said to himself, "It must be a trick! That's it! They are not being affected because there isn't any radiation. They've messed with the sensors and disabled the cameras so that the core is really shut down tight and they aren't getting any radiation. Well, I will fix their wagons right now." He stormed out of the control room and down to the core room airlock. The outer door would not open because the inner one was still open. Ivan pushed the manual override button to disable the interlock between the doors. When one of the technicians tried to stop him, he backhanded the tech so that he flew across the room. "These guys are not going to make a fool out of me!"

Ivan cranked open the outer door and charged through the airlock into the core room. He had his gun out but stopped still when he saw the fourth man in the room. Ivan dropped his gun said, "No, you are not real". For several seconds he stood there staring and then he turned and ran back out of the airlock.

Jack, Mark, and Victor walked out of the airlock and it closed and latched by itself. They walked out of the containment building into the walkway back to the missile control room singing songs of praise to the Son of Yahveh. They stopped and looked around. They were outdoors and the last thing they remembered they were in the core room. Jack automatically looked at his watch and saw that twenty minutes had gone by and he didn't feel sick or anything. As it dawned on him that Yahveh had protected them from the radiation he dropped to his knees and thanked Yahveh from the bottom of his heart. The other two men joined him. After praying his thanks Jack stood up and saw three of the guards running away from him.

Mark said next to him, "They think we're either ghosts or radioactive."

Jack nodded, "Let's see if we can use that idea to help us get the girls out of their bondage."

As the three of them walked off toward the mansion, the sadistic Ivan, alone in the forest, cried to himself, "No, no, no!" As he felt blood start leaking out of his nose and then out of his mouth. He knew what was happening to him. He remembered doing to others. Then his vision blurred and everything went black. Ivan heard the most evil laugh he'd ever heard and knew that he was lost forever. His pitiful wail went unheard.

CHAPTER TWENTY-FIVE

As Jack approached the mansion, Victor reached up and tapped him on the shoulder. Jack looked at the man that built the mansion and followed him into a small garden with a large fountain against the building at the end of the garden. Victor reached into the spray on the fountain and moved one of the cherubs there. The large stone wall surrounding the fountain slid noiselessly aside and there was a doorway with a combination lock set into the wall. Victor tapped in a code and they were in the mansion without running into any guards.

Jack asked where they would probably take the women. Before Victor could answer there was a scream from down the hall. Victor raised one eyebrow and suggestively pointed in that direction. All three men ran down the hall until they clearly heard the sound of grunts and a struggle. Jack opened the door and stepped into the room followed closely by Mark and Victor.

The room was a shambles. The furniture was broken and strewn around, and the drapes hung cockeyed from one window and were gone from the next. In the middle of the room stood Laura and Sarah, back-to-back, with a circle of six men surrounding them. More impressive was the piles of men, their bodies scattered around. There had to be at least eight men either unconscious or dead on the floor. The remaining six men looked really haggard and unsure.

The largest man said to the man next to him. "The @%$&* with this! I say if they won't cooperate then we just shoot them and throw their bodies into the ocean. No woman is worth this much trouble." He reached for his pistol and found Mark's massive hand already gripping it. He tried to turn around but was suddenly picked up from the floor and slammed down onto the floor head first. The crunch of shattered bone was loud. The man died with a broken neck as Mark turned the pistol on the other men.

Two other men went for their handguns only to lose the shootout to Mark. The other three men held their hands up over their heads.

Mark told them to run and not stop until they got to the mainland. They left as quickly as their legs would let them. While Victor kept an eye on the dead, unconscious, and badly wounded troops, Jack and Mark hugged their wives. Sarah was still ready to fight anybody. She expressed her gladness to see both men still alive and well, especially Mark. Then she stooped and picked up two pistols from fallen bodies and started looking for someone to shoot. Mark wisely let her go about her own form of cooling down.

Laura told them that the group of underlings were supposed to make her and Sarah docile for the directors. The men had underestimated the combat capabilities of either woman but especially that of the ex-Mossad operative. Laura said that Sarah kicked, hacked, punched, and generally destroyed five of the men in the first sixty seconds. Then she and Laura managed to disable three more rather severely before Mark and Jack joined the party. Jack hugged her again and told her he was impressed with both of them and their fighting abilities. She smiled and reminded him that Yahveh was their protector.

Anyway, Laura said that she thought she saw a flash of silver and gold in the middle of the battle. Then she looked at Jack with a quizzical eyebrow raised, "But, my armor didn't appear at all!"

Jack thought about that. "It's probably because the battle was basically a physical one and not a spiritual one."

She nodded, and then she asked, "I am really happy that it didn't turn out that way, but, how come you're not a melting gob of radioactive goo?"

Jack smiled, "Same Yahveh. Yahshua protected us from the radiation and I believe that the Holy Spirit spoke through me and condemned Lallatun and his buddies to a death of that same radiation poisoning. Sort of like when the Pharaoh threatened to kill all the first born of the Jews and Yahveh allowed him to pronounce the death sentence on the entire first born of Egypt. I will tell you that the three of us were in the company of Yahshua in that containment building and I really wish you could have been there. He turned a fatal situation into a most wonderful one. I don't think I've ever experienced anything like that."

Laura hugged him again, "That's all right. He's been with us all today."

By then, Sarah had returned from her hunt without any new victims but only slightly relaxed. She stuffed the two pistols into her waistband and asked Mark. "Okay, Mr. Fix-it, what made you smile about that rocket? It headed west like it was headed for Israel."

Seeing the dark look he was getting from his wife, Mark smiled, "No, not really. It did head west, but it didn't go to Israel."

"Where did it go then?"

"Well, when I got to the guidance system I found they had adapted a new laser seeker head to the missile, so I rewired it so that the seeker head would lock onto the brightest source of infrared light, which in this case is the sun. The missile headed west because after it had climbed about a thousand feet or so, it detected the setting sun and realigned itself to attack the sun."

Jack asked, "Did it have enough boost to escape the Earth's gravitational pull?"

Mark nodded, "You bet, and, it will use the fourth stage, the liquid fueled one, to make adjustments to keep it on course for the whole trip. By the time it left the atmosphere it already had exceeded the planet's gravitational pull and after it reached space it probably added about another hundred and fifty thousand miles per hour to its flight speed before the fourth stage ran out of solid fuel."

Victor shook his head, "ICBMs don't have that kind of propellant or range."

Mark laughed, "You're right, normally. But what these guys didn't know when they stole this one is that it was one of ten that had been converted to test vehicles to see if they could be reused as a delivery vehicle for interplanetary missions. The range modifications were made to the fourth, third, and second stages with the lift-off stage, stage one, basically the same. The terrorists would have been surprised to see that it cleared the atmosphere before the second stage even began to burn. The Air Force used an experimental solid fuel propellant that had a burn rate about eight times as long as the original. I would say that the bomb is going to reach a speed of somewhere in the area of 200,000 M.P.H. and add almost nothing to the sun, which is the largest sustained thermonuclear explosion in this part of the universe."

Victor computed the speed and distance in his head and announced, "It will reach the vicinity of the sun in about nineteen days but will burn up way before it gets to the chromosphere."

Jack liked the rocket solution but suggested that they find some way to get some friendly troops onto the island and some nuclear control teams too. In the meantime they needed to find out where the opposition was and what they are planning.

Sarah asked, "You mean the rulers of this little part of hell?"

"No, I mean the guards here and any other low life's that have come to these shores. I sincerely believe that Yahveh will take care of Lallatun and his cronies."

The next several hours were spent seeking the enemy. Very few were found. It was like the rats had deserted the ship...but why?

Victor found an answer on the communications net inside the mansion. It seems that the leaders dispersed, heading back for their home bases. This left the guards to face whatever retribution would be coming from Israel for the missile strike. It was clear that the Israelis would be able to pinpoint the launch point by satellite within minutes of the launch.

One of the captured guards explained that the cannon fodder had no intention of being on the receiving end of a return nuclear strike so they had also fled the island leaving the islanders to fend for each other. Only the occasional straggler who didn't make the boat was still on the island and scared to death. They would be easy to round up.

Upon Sarah's suggestion, Victor contacted the U.S. Government and she contacted the Mossad for support on the island. The U.S. was sending a combat nuclear containment force as well as troops.

Mark's contact with the U.S. Navy resolved some of NORAD's concerns about the launch and they were also sending a team to determine how the people who displaced Victor were able to secure and deliver the modified Peacemaker missile.

In his personal luxury jet, Hiram Lallatun was irritated. He had been listening to the world broadcasts for reaction to the strike on Israel for the last sixty minutes. There were no mentions of anything. He thought they might be covering up the strike to prevent world panic. He was still celebrating when something fell past his eyes into his lap. He reached down and found a handful of hair, his hair. He felt something running down his chin from the corner of his mouth. He reached up and saw the bright red color on his fingers. About that time his vision began to blur and it struck him that he was dying of radiation poisoning even though he had left the island before they had opened the containment building. He began to feel the pain inside and outside as the terrible onslaught of the radiation began to destroy him. In an absent-minded way he wondered why his mind hadn't gone yet. For him, it would be the last thing to pass away and he was going to be allowed to feel all the pain. Then things would get much worse for him. He made a little moan of pain but no one could hear him.

On other ships and planes, the same fate was leveled against the other five directors' of the group.

Later, the medical authorities were baffled by the deaths because they couldn't trace them to a source. It was like each of the men had been fully exposed to a source of powerful radioactivity.

CHAPTER TWENTY-SIX

The fate of several of the directors of Lallatun's group was news by the time the first contingent of agents, troops, and scientists arrived on Victor Chamberlain's island. Chamberlain essentially gave physical and legal ownership of the far side of his island to the U.S. nuclear and military teams. At his mansion he, and the rest of the team spent two days being 'debriefed' by authorities of all kinds.

At Mark's request the President of the United States invoked a Presidential Privilege Coverage for the five people and they were all allowed to leave for the U.S. Victor traveled with the four team members and ended up at Castle Malone as an honored guest. One who, incidentally, got to help with the dishes every now and then and couldn't have been happier.

On the fourth day after their return, the new replacement for the Connelly's armored SUV was being brought to the house in Denver when it was attacked and run off of the road. A local Sheriff's deputy saw the attack and called for backup. The attackers had fled before they could get at the driver in the vehicle. All this was reported to Jack at his house by the Sheriff himself.

Calling a meeting Jack sat down in front of his friends and laid out the question. "What in Sam Hill is going on? Weren't the attacks before we went to the island orchestrated by Lallatun and his gang?"

Mark, deep in thought, commented, "Doesn't look like it unless this is some kind of revenge for the demise of the 'directors'."

Laura threw up her arms. "Doesn't this stuff ever stop?"

The phone rang and Jack answered it. "Hello?"

The voice on the other end of the phone was obviously electronically altered. "Malone. You will turn over the crucifixion nail to us at a place to be chosen or you and your family, and friends, will die. Do you unders..."

Jack hung up the phone and sighed. "Now it's threatening phone calls." After checking the Caller ID and finding 'anonymous', he walked over to the sofa and sat down heavily. "I want to pray for a while. I want to see if the Holy Spirit will give us some insight on this continual warfare." With that he leaned back and closed his eyes and began praying quietly in his prayer language.

Laura went over to the couch and joined him. The other three left the room and decided to use whatever normal channels of information they could to see if they could add to the understanding of this battle.

After a while of praising the Lord and then prayer about the attacks, Jack entered into a peaceful place and rested there, quietly, waiting to see what Yahveh's answer would be to his questions.

No answers, no angels, just a deep peace and a conviction that Yahveh was in charge and things were going to work out all right. Opening his eyes he found Laura sitting quietly next to him, still in prayer.

Jack thought over the situation and realized that the earlier attacks, without the two demonic elements, the large guy and the black cloud, were as well planned in their lethal intent as were the efforts of Lallatun and his crew. The attacks were very professional and organized in planning but not in execution. In hindsight he compared the overall various attacks and their supposed aim and effects.

They had attacked the house, apparently to get the nail. They had tried to kill Sarah and had tried to kidnap him at the Dojo, presumably to accomplish the same mission. They tried to either kill or kidnap his father in the mountains, the Sensei at the airport and the Minister at his church. They had been lured to Victor's island primarily to get the nail. Now the enemy had mistakenly attacked the Connelly's new SUV in an apparent attempt to kill them again. So, the forces arrayed against them wanted the Malones and the nail but were also intent on destroying all their support.

Add to that the list of people the enemy was hunting for and it all pointed back to the time in Denver when this all started with the Don Miland gang. It looked like one control and a bunch of different agents or groups trying to accomplish a single goal.

But who was behind it? They had looked at the remaining bad guys from the Denver time and basically only had the demonic force that had the necessary information about the nail. At least, he was the only real enemy survivor of that encounter. Of course the renegade policeman, John Dalman had several weeks before he died in Chicago in a gun battle with a local gang. He could have had another partner. But that didn't feel right. No, it was something more, something bigger than a single demon or Dalman. But what was it? His train of thought was interrupted by the ringing of the telephone. Sighing, Jack got up and answered it.

The caller was Laura's friend from the CBI. They had no information that would shed any light on the attacks and the people involved with the attacks had all simply disappeared. Several had bench warrants out for them for not appearing in court but they were missing.

Three weeks later there had been no additional attacks. The leads had all been followed and the investigation had reached a dead end. There were no new revelations from heaven concerning these things and things began to look less dangerous. Mark and Sarah received a request from the U.S. Government for an investigation into a terrorist-related accident in Greece and left to manage that business.

The days after Christmas were cold and snowy in the Denver area but with the lack of aggression the days opened up to normal living for the Malones. Jack began spending his time at Technological Alternatives working on new projects. He made time each day for prayer and sought the direction of the Lord in everything he did.

Laura quickly became bored with the inactivity and originally thought of returning to a position with the financial management company she had worked for but she really didn't feel led to do that. Her prayer time with the Lord led her to volunteer her time at various charities and agencies that took care of the aged.

They spent time together and honed their martial arts skills and worked out by target shooting, exercising, and mountain biking. For Jack and Laura, the first six months of the New Year were a quiet, laconic season after the year of excitement they had lived through.

One day in June, Jack and Laura had decided to take a short vacation and visit Mark and Sarah in London where they were working on a nasty case of multiple murders tied into world terrorism. It was a typical day in London at the upscale hotel where they were sitting down to lunch the day they arrived. It was raining and dark and overcast.

Glad to see their friends again, Mark and Sarah talked excitedly about the things they had been doing. When Mark explained the case they were on Jack recognized the feelings he was experiencing. He felt left out and it was obvious that Laura was missing the action too. Jack listened to the tales of intrigue and espionage and then asked, "Do you two need our help? We're becoming a normal couple again and frankly, it's boring."

Mark looked at Sarah and grinned. "Sure, we could use your help. They outlined the problems they were having and Jack and Laura added what insight they could. It was an exciting three weeks and while not up to the levels of danger and non-stop action they had experienced, it was good to be working side-by-side with Mark and Sarah again. It was as if they had begun to really live again.

When the case was completed, the four of them returned to Castle Malone in Denver. A week later, Jack's father called and asked Jack and Laura to come up to the new church in the mountains. Mark and Sarah were off visiting some friends in from Israel so Jack accepted the invitation and headed for the mountains.

CHAPTER TWENTY-SEVEN

Jack drove slowly up the driveway to the church. The magnificent Rocky Mountains spread out behind and above the small structure in the afternoon sun in a riot of color and granite grays. The parking lot was set into a natural cave-like sheltered area that was open on three sides. The roof of the garage was hewn out of the natural rock and looked just like the surrounding terrain with small pines and Aspens along with shrubs growing on it. The openings let light and air into the area but protected vehicles from the wind, weather, and future snowfalls. While there was room for roughly one hundred cars there was only one there right then.

Jack parked near his dad's car and he and Laura got out and walked over the flagstone walk to the front doors of the church. The building itself was set into a granite wall. It almost looked as if the church had been hollowed into the cliff itself. The granite was dressed across its length and was designed to draw attention to the large cross which was in bas-relief from the ground to a height of sixty feet just twenty feet to the right of the doors. It was an extremely good example of the stonecutter's craftsmanship which would endure for centuries.

The doors opened pneumatically as they approached and silently closed behind them after they had moved into the foyer. Jack recognized the interior design as similar to their new home. It was alike in the tasteful color selections and the use of aroma and lighting to accent the decor. He also felt the lift supplied by ion generators. The sound was muted in the foyer which had three sets of double doors leading to the sanctuary and several others to the sides of the room.

Steve Malone came out of one of the side doors and waved at them across the fifty foot space. "Come on over here", he called. They walked over and he led them through the solid six-panel relief door into the office space for the church. There were several small conference rooms and sub-office rooms off of the main area and two reception desks for daily business. They were the only ones there since the church's grand opening was scheduled for that weekend.

Steve showed them around the office which was leading-edge, state-of-the-art with computer controls and flat-panel computer displays everywhere. The person, or people, in here could see and control every area of the church from the gate at the highway to the baptistery water level and temperature.

Laura asked, "Aren't you worried that the remote location will entice some people to attempt to steal this equipment?"

Steve laughed, "Laura, you forget where your husband got his precautionary nature. This entire establishment is guarded by a second generation NovaStar system and there is a Sheriff's office six miles away that is on-call. Even if no one is here, the NovaStar system will summon help to arrest the captives. During the weekends we have contracted with the Deputies for off-duty service with full pay and benefits. They have been providing protection for us since there were only six trailers parked up here eight months ago. Three of them have signed up as members of the church and actually donate their time as ushers during the services. We also have the full-time recording capabilities of the NovaStar system linked to the CBI database for automatic criminal identification. This is explained in our brochures and on a sign that will be posted in the garage. There is no reason to think that the few things we have here will make a criminal action worth the exposure and effort."

Jack laughed quietly and asked his father. "So the NovaStar system will catch thieves? I thought Christian churches were supposed to free the captives."

Steve smiled ruefully, "We do! We release them to the police for the proper guidance and admonishment." That presented a mental picture that made them all laugh.

Steve then showed them the other rooms off of the foyer which contained a large reception hall which could be reconfigured into several smaller conference or party rooms. Attached to that was a fully-equipped kitchen with all the latest equipment such as walk-in freezers and refrigerators, state of the artranges, natural gas ovens, an automatic commercial dish washer, and food preparation and storage areas. The kitchen was lit by natural light through the Portal system Steve had designed for commercial use in houses like Castle Malone. It was interesting to have a large window expanse of thirty feet showing a beautiful valley when you knew there was the entire office complex between you and the view.

The other rooms provided storage and equipment rooms for the systems that maintained the church. Jack noted the large electrical control panel in the power room and asked, "Wind and solar?"

Steve grinned, "Yep! We've got three horizontal wind turbines set back into the cliff face about ninety feet from the church that supply over ten kilowatts of power constantly and a proprietary storage system that stores the electricity they generate. There is also a solar farm on the top of the area out of sight that can generate about sixty percent of the wind turbine input as a backup. With the constant wind we have through the valley and across the face of the cliff there is no shortage of power. In fact, we sell three times more power back to the electric company than we would consume on a daily basis."

After seeing all the supporting rooms and systems, Steve led them into the sanctuary. The doors opened by sliding back into the walls so that no one would run into them when they were open. Again it was operated by pneumatic power and totally silent.

Jack and Laura looked around the room. There were approximately two hundred cushioned seats, similar to those in a modern movie theater, arranged in tiered rows. Each tier was lower than the one behind it providing for an excellent view for everyone of the podium and altar area. The rows were separated by a central aisle and two other aisles dividing the remainder of the seats into four areas. The seats were large, plush, and comfortable and had armrests that could be pulled down like an aircraft seat. The armrests contained a small writing surface that could be opened out to allow for note taking or to rest a Bible on.

The ceiling and floor were a translucent light-gray, marble-like surface as were the side walls and the large wall behind the podium. In contrast, the back wall in which the three doors were set was native granite rock. The inside of the doors were a matching granite surface that blended into the wall when closed so that the entire back surface resembled a granite wall.

The three aisles were carpeted with royal Maroon-Red carpets that led from the doors down to the presentation platform and podium at the front. The platform was also made of the translucent marble surface except where the podium was which was carpeted like the aisles. There were no windows or pictures set into the walls in the softly lit interior. The majority of the floor, ceiling and walls were a translucent pearl gray. It was a restful but somewhat bland setting.

Steve had them sit in the front row and smiled at them. "Understand that this church has been built with Yahveh's money, for the purpose of praising Him, and that you are completely in Yahveh's hands while you're here."

At that he touched a control on the podium, the ceiling, floor, and walls disappeared completely and everything changed. To the eye, the chairs, podium, and aisle carpeting were freely suspended over two hundred feet of empty space with the noontime sky above them and the beautiful valley spread out below and in front of them. Even Jack grabbed the armrests in surprise and anticipation of falling. He saw the look on his father's face and knew that he had generated the right reaction. The effect was totally believable with a breeze blowing across the chairs that gently ruffled Laura's hair and the sounds of the valley bouncing off of the cliff and registering as echoes in just the right timing. A bird, on the way home to its nest, flew by the back of the podium and eyed them as it went by. Jack half expected it to fly through the church seating area but it stayed behind his father as it whipped by.

Laura looked back at the rear wall and saw a solid granite wall with the three carpets leading up to the camouflaged doors. The sunlight was in the right position and shadows were where they would be normally if there was no roof, walls, or floor to the church sanctuary. The effect was complete and with the sounds and breeze it was impossible to tell that you weren't actually just hanging off of the canyon wall. To all intents and purposes the carpeted aisles, the chairs, and the podium were actually suspended out from the cliff.

After experiencing the effect for a few minutes Jack stood up, stepped off of the carpeting onto nothing it seemed, and then walked up the carpet to the podium. Squatting down, he examined the part of the platform that wasn't covered with carpeting. It was also an absolute illusion. He could feel the platform but couldn't focus his eyes on it.

He grinned and stood up; walking up on the platform he looked back across the sanctuary and noticed that the illusion held up from that view too, even though he knew they were surrounded by rock walls. When the illusion was in effect, the lighting was supplied by the natural sunlight and there were shadows wherever there was a physically visible surface to show up. There were no shadows on the floor below the chairs which would have jarred the illusion. Looking around Jack agreed with his father's statement. You really did feel that you were in the hand of Yahveh and suspended in midair.

Steve restored the room view and explained the operation. "We have view sensors out on struts beyond the canyon wall. These are the views you see when the projectors are on. The microphone pickups and wind sensors are out there too so that we replicate the wind with fans and the light is supplied through the portals. Now, for you I did the instant transformation. This is how it will normally be handled for the less adventurous." He touched two controls and the room slowly faded from sight to be replaced by the outside illusion over the span of a full minute. It didn't take away from the illusion but did give one time to adapt to the change.

Laura laughed. "I don't know. I think the quick way is the best. Although I agree that some older people or people with heart conditions might have a problem with the switch that seems to put them in jeopardy."

Jack asked his dad, "What if someone walks on the surface where there is no carpet. Doesn't it scuff up and lose some of the illusion?"

Steve nodded his head, "Yes it would somewhat. We are using an experimental surface here that is transparent but extremely inert and resistant to scratching. I think it will hold up, but, if it does get damaged, we can repair it seamlessly."

Laura came up to the podium. "Okay, this would definitely keep people aware of their dependence on Yahveh. Who do you have as a speaker?"

Steve looked at his watch. "You'll meet the first Minister in few minutes." As he spoke the central set of doors opened in the rear wall and Larry Malone walked into the sanctuary. He came down to the podium and hugged the three people there.

Laura smiled and said, "You're just in time to meet the new preacher."

Larry nodded, "Yes, I know, that would be me."

Jack looked at his uncle with surprise. "When did you become a minister of Yahveh?"

Larry set his Bible on the lectern and spread his hands. "Ever since Steve and I were born again I've been urged by Yahveh's Holy Spirit to take up the call to preach the word of Yahveh to the lost. Over the last four years I have taken the courses and passed the tests and was ordained this year. I have actually been preaching in Marlin for over a year." Marlin was a small, predominately Mexican community just south of Waco, Texas where Larry's wife had family.

Jack smiled and shook his hand. "Congratulations. I guess I had bettered not include you on any more assaults?"

Larry shook his head, "I don't think so, but don't count me out if Yahveh wants me there. I follow the leading of the Lord. This occupation is at His bidding and if He wants me to be a minister that takes a physical role in resisting the devil, He'll let me know."

They talked for a while and then Jack and Laura headed back to Denver with a great impression of the church in the mountains. It was almost a miracle and should draw substantial crowds after the announcement by several of the news media in the State of Colorado. The second day after the initial blessing and opening of the church, Steve had invited pastors and ministers from all over to a special time of prayer and had been assured of a full house. It would keep him busy for quite a while.

CHAPTER TWENTY-EIGHT

As they headed down from the interstate 70 tunnel past El Rancho on their way to Denver, Jack noticed a pattern in the traffic around them. At first he attributed it to his imagination and desire for action. But casually watching the large black semitrailer in front of them and two cars that were slowly hemming the SUV in from the sides and heavy tow truck at their rear, he was fairly sure that their time of peace had come to an end. He looked over at his wife and said, "Honey, I think our break is over. Would you get the hand-guns out of the lockup under the seat?"

Laura grinned and reached down and pressed the right combination of buttons and the door to the locked compartment slid open. She took the two Ruger P-90 45-calibre automatics out of the safe and slid one to Jack across the console. Jack reached out and casually depressed the EWANS panic button that would notify Mark and Sarah that they had encountered some form of hostility.

Thanks to a slower car in the right lane that made the blocker on that side fall back, Jack saw his chance and pulled to the right and accelerated along side of the semi. The four vehicle team wasn't sure they had been made or not so they didn't go into panic mode but just kept pace with the SUV so that they could box it in again farther down the mountainside. Jack wasn't going to let them control the situation so he accelerated again and passed the semitrailer completely. He made it look like he was simply doing what came naturally to keep the enemy off balance. He also wanted to make sure this was a snatch and grab effort and not simply an over-active imagination on his part.

That decision was made fairly quickly as the semi and the car sped up to re-establish the rolling box around the SUV. Laura kept the other vehicles in sight in her sun visor mirror and used her cell phone to call the Arapahoe County Sheriff's department's 9-1-1 number. She explained that there were several vehicles that were attempting to prevent their getting to Denver and were actively attacking them. The Sheriff's department began to dispatch officers toward their area.

Obviously someone in the enemy vehicles had a police scanner and knew that they had been detected. But, instead of breaking and feigning innocence, as they still could have done, they went for the SUV with a vengeance. Expecting that result from Laura's phone call, Jack had kept an eye on the Semi. When it started to gather speed, well in excess of the speed limit, Jack mashed the accelerator in the powerful SUV and surged ahead of the group. By now they were nearing 100 miles per hour and beginning to encounter conflicts with other traffic. As they screamed down the I-70 corridor toward Arvada, one of the Arapahoe County Sheriff's cars joined the melee. Then, not one but two, police helicopters flew into position above the speeding group. But it seemed that the attackers did not care about the involvement of the police as they pushed even harder and faster to box in the Cadillac SUV.

At this point Jack was in the right lane and the semi had come up alongside in the middle lane. The two blocking cars were in front of Jack and the semitrailer with only the tow truck behind him. Jack took a chance and suddenly veered to the right and took the Genesee Ridge Road/South Grapevine Road exit. This effectively cut off three-fourths of the pursuit and left them to the police. The tow truck made the exit behind the SUV and slowed behind it as Jack brought the chase to a halt a half mile from the exit. One of the police helicopters had stayed with them as they made the break and now hovered over the two vehicles. A loud speaker told everyone to exit their vehicles with their hands in plain sight.

Sliding the automatic into his belt under his jacket, Jack slowly climbed out of the SUV with Laura matching him on the other side. They each held their hands out where the police could see them. No one was getting out of the tow truck even though the police repeated their demands.

Jack heard the revving of the truck's engine and was ready as it accelerated toward him. Throwing himself forward and past the front of the SUV he dodged away from the truck which then sped by him and headed down the side road with the helicopter in pursuit.

Laura came over to him and smiled. "Just like old times, right? I'm actually glad because I thought I would like the peace and quiet. But enough of anything is enough. She pulled the automatic out of her purse and de-cocked it and put the safety back on. She was about to put it back in her purse when there was a fairly good-sided explosion about a mile up the side road and smoke could be seen growing in a column. Jack couldn't see the police helicopter anymore. This didn't bode well if the attackers took out a helicopter. He tipped his head as a signal and they quickly got back in the SUV. Just as he started to pull out his cell phone signaled an incoming call.

Mark was on the phone. Jack filled him in on the developing situation as he made a small, cross-country trek and was able to regain the Interstate highway headed for Denver. Mark told him that the Air Force was bringing him a helicopter in a few minutes and he would fly directly to wherever the SUV was when he could get there for air support. Jack said that they would leave the EWANS signal on as a position lock.

As they drove by the column of smoke off of the right hand side of the interstate they could see between the cars of the on-lookers that the helicopter was indeed down and burning on the ground. But, the tow truck was also burning a few dozen feet away from the charred wreckage of the helicopter. Laura couldn't see anyone moving near either crash site.

Laura's cell phone chirped and she answered it to hear the 9-1-1 operator asking her to go to a specific mile marker on I-70 to meet with Sheriff's department officers there. When she asked what was happening, the operator would not give her any details, only that the Sheriff's department needed them at that mile marker immediately.

Something in Jack's spirit bridled at the summons and he dialed 9-1-1 on his cell phone. After thirty seconds he determined that whoever was talking to Laura were not official 9-1-1 personnel. He could tell from the green signs on the side of the interstate that they were less than two miles from the one Laura's contact was demanding they go to. When he saw two wrecked Sheriff's cars by the left-hand side of the interstate he realized that their opposition wasn't worried about collateral damage or killing police to get to them. He was going to pull over and stop before getting to the designated mile marker when the SUV was rammed from behind.

Irritated that he had dropped his guard in that direction, Jack floored the SUV and pulled away from the pick-up truck that was behind them. The pick-up was a new vehicle and had enough power to match the SUV. He attempted to ram them again but Jack swung to the right side and slammed on the brakes. The pickup shot by and then started smoking its tires to slow down. Something started hammering on the right side of the SUV and Laura ducked down towards the console as a flurry of automatic rifle fire struck that side. Jack looked to his right and saw another SUV with two guys firing rifles out the side windows at them.

By now the normal traffic had either stopped to avoid the melee or raced away from them towards Denver.

The pickup tried to swerve in front of the Cadillac but was still going too fast and almost lost it with the two right hand wheels off the ground. The driver was skilled enough to save it by counter-steering but wobbled far to the left hand side of the highway in an attempt to stay upright.

Jack took advantage of their mistake to accelerate away from them as the entire rolling warfare came into Lakewood on the west side of Denver. Several more Sheriff's cars and two Lakewood Police cars got involved and almost as quickly were sidelined by heavy rifle fire from three different vehicles.

Jack saw three other vehicles attempting to block the interstate at the mile marker Laura had been told to go to. He jockeyed the SUV to get by the enemy vehicles.About that time one of the vehicles with guns converged on their SUV. Jack bounced the car to the right with the side of the bigger SUV and the shooters spun out of action to the right.

Laura screamed and Jack instinctively hit the brakes. A 40mm grenade round sailed over the hood of the SUV with only inches to spare from hitting the windshield. It impacted on a bridge abutment to the left of the highway and exploded. Jack couldn't tell if anyone was hurt or not. The frenetic pace of events was demanding his complete focus. He was praying in his mind that Yahshua would protect them.

All at once four of the attacking vehicles blew up in violent explosions that completely destroyed the vehicles and anyone inside them. Parts of cars, and pickup trucks flew off in all directions. One of the tires from a car bounced off the SUV and an exploding gas tank threw flaming gasoline onto the left-rear quarter panel of the Malone's vehicle. Two more massive explosions behind them shook their teeth but also finished off the road block, leaving only one of the identifiable opposing vehicles intact. It was rapidly being surrounded by police cars and a SWAT team.

Coming to a halt in the middle of the interstate with fires all around them the Malones watched as the pickup that had been attacking them rolled slowly by with the cab and engine compartment gutted and burning violently. The new pickup was not much more than four wheels which had miraculously survived the explosion and a bed of fire. The remains of the pickup rolled over to the edge of the highway and stopped when it hit the barrier to the west bound lanes. Jack reached up and carefully pressed the EWANS button again to disable the signal. Laura looked at him and they said in unison, "Mark's here!"

Another explosion destroyed the remaining enemy vehicle causing police and SWAT members to seek shelter anywhere they could. At that point a relative form of quiet settled down over the area. Flashing lights and strident sirens still filled the air as dozens of emergency and police vehicles came rushing towards them from all directions with lights flashing rapidly in several colors. But, even the police moved aside as a heavily armed Apache AH-64XV combat helicopter settled to the highway a hundred feet from the SUV on the interstate. The gray tell-tale residue from the missile racks indicated where the firepower had come from that ended the running fight. Mark jumped from the helicopter while the pilot kept an eye on the area for more hostiles.

Mark jogged over to them and checked to see that they were all right and then went to talk to the various officers that were starting to flood into the battleground.

In a repeat of his earlier performance, Mark convinced all involved that the Malones were to accompany him out of the area. Since an AH-64 only holds a crew of two, a second helicopter arrived to ferry the Malones with Sarah in command. It was the fully-armed MH-53J Pavelow III combat helicopter that had responded to the attack on Sarah. As the helicopter lifted off of the highway Jack surveyed the forlorn-looking SUV with all the pock-marks and burns marring the once beautiful white-pearl finish. It would take considerable time to repair their sturdy conveyance. The armored and modified Cadillac had done well, all things considering. But he was still glad that the 40mm grenade hadn't hit them. That would have really messed things up.

Thirty minutes later the four of them reached Castle Malone and relaxed for the first time since Jack noticed the rolling road block in the mountains.

CHAPTER TWENTY-NINE

"All right...we need to figure out what happened today, what it means, and how to prevent things like this in the future." Jack looked at the other six people in the living room to make sure they understood what he wanted to achieve. "I intend to bring this reign of terror to an end! Have no doubts about this. We are going to focus strictly on who is behind these attacks and put them out of business, permanently!" His anger and frustration were evident but also evident was his determination to reach the stated goal.

In addition to Laura, Mark, and Sarah at the meeting that night were Jack and Mark's Sensei, Jim Grady, who had connections from his twenty years of active duty as a Denver Police Sergeant. Jack marveled that over the years he had known the man he still looked a great deal like a champion wrestler in build and the fire in his eyes had not dimmed since his youth.

Next to him sat Minister Throman, The next seat was occupied by Carol Nolan, a pretty brunette that was nearing her thirties but looked like she could still be in high school. She was an agent of the Colorado Bureau of Investigation or CBI. Her life with the Malones and Mark Connelly started when they were able to save her from torture by Don Miland while they were attempting to clear the Malones of false charges. During that rescue, both she and Sensei Grady had been present when a demon tried to possess the crucifixion nail and was confronted and rebuked by Yahshua himself. That event in the basement of Don Miland's mansion forever changed all of their lives and created a bond between all of them that time would never break. Jack asked Mark to bring the newcomers, Carol, and Sensei Grady, up to speed on the latest attack.

Mark got up and described the initial attempt to box in the SUV, the chase, the side road escape, and the departure of the tow truck past the SUV. "They wanted to draw the police helicopter away from the SUV because they had other assets they wanted to bring into play. Jack messed them up when he went cross country and back onto the interstate. Then the people in the tow truck decided to eliminate the helicopter. They apparently shot it down with a Russian rocket-propelled grenade, an RPG. The pilot, who lived to tell the tale, had recently flown combat in Iraq and wasn't too pleased by their destroying his whirly-bird. So he controlled the crash so that he was able to drop the back of the chopper on the truck and then bail out his side door. The truck then crashed and caught fire next to the burning chopper. The only people dead in this action were the three men in the tow truck. The pilot was alone when the RPG hit his aircraft." Mark took a drink of his coffee and then continued.

"By this time Jack and Laura were eastbound again on I-70 and the enemy decided to up the ante and build their own roadblock. Simultaneously they tried to imitate the 9-1-1 operator and direct the SUV to the roadblock. We assume that their orders were to capture the Malones regardless of the collateral damages or interference by the police. This also indicates that the enemy has the resources to determine cell phone numbers as well as the Malone's schedule. I would suspect some kind of phone tap. They knew when you were going to Steve's church and approximately when you'd be headed back."

"Jack figured out the ruse and was attempting to run past the road block when the opposing forces decided to bring the SUV down regardless of the possible damage to the occupants. They fired a 40mm, rifle-launched grenade at the SUV but missed. That brings us up to when I got there.

Mark clicked on the display for the laptop computer. The 60" TV came to life and Mark continued explaining the action by matching his comments to the video. "What you are seeing here is the military gun cameras on the Apache helicopter." He slowed the action down and pointed out the missile launches and the resultant explosions of the first four vehicles and then the second launch and the destruction of the other two. It was sobering to see how quickly the military system locked on, fired, and destroyed the six cars and pickup trucks. The camera turned on the last enemy vehicle but no missile was launched as the police surrounded the car. The car simply blew up on its own.

Mark shook his head. "We wanted to leave someone alive so we could find out what they knew. We didn't do the last one, they did it to themselves. The video ended as the chopper landed on the highway.

Carol got up and gave Mark a 1" DVD. "Play this," she said. She stood there as the second video of the chase took place on the TV screen. "This is a copy of the official CBI helicopter video of the chase. They use these videos to build investigations and to provide backup for court cases. They were in the right place at the right time."

The assembled group watched as the chase was over flown by both helicopters and picked up as Jack swung off at the exit. The events unfolded in full color and sound. The CBI chopper had stayed with the black semi and the other police cars on the interstate while the Colorado Highway Patrol helicopter went with Jack's SUV and the tow truck.

Nothing in the final stages was different from the black and white gun camera recording except that it was in color with full stereo sound and from a different angle that allowed the viewers to watch the missile launches from the Apache and the resultant destruction on the ground.

As the TV was turned off, Sensei Grady got up and added the conclusions the combined police forces had reached so far. "There has been no viable identification of either any of the involved vehicles or the people that were in them. The vehicles were most likely stolen and the shooters probably will have no identification on them. This was set up by professionals but carried out by less skilled operatives. There were at least twenty-three people involved and the body count at present is twenty-one. The two people in the semitrailer truck escaped. The truck was found abandoned on the interstate a half mile before the place of the roadblock. There were so many civilian, non-involved vehicles that the police did not notice this one as being the truck involved prior to that. There were three policemen seriously hurt and hospitalized but none killed."

Sensei Grady looked at the others in the room. "This little fracas was seen on national TV this evening. Two other helicopters were there, higher up. One of them was Channel 2 Television. They got into the chase three miles before the road block and proceeded to air the whole bloody mess before anyone could stop them.

Mark sat there for a few seconds. "What about the other chopper? Was it a news chopper?"

Jim thought for a second, "No, there was no other coverage than that of Channel 2."

Mark slapped the table he was sitting beside. "I'll bet you dollars to doughnuts that other chopper was a control and communications chopper for the bad guys!"

He got up and grabbed his cell phone. Sensei Grady looked at him quizzically. "Your video and that of the CBI didn't get a glimpse of the higher helicopters. How do we get a fix on the one the bad guys might have been using?"

Mark smiled and held up his left hand for silence. "This is General Connelly; I would like to speak to the facility commander immediately please." While he waited he explained. "We are not the only ones with eyes you know. Not that the NSA or the other alphabet agencies would be looking at this particular place and time but its worth a shot to see if any of the satellites were imaging that piece of the world right then.

After getting the commander's permission he explained to the tech running the search, "I need an identification of a civilian helicopter that was operating at..." he read off the GPS coordinates from the Apache location system, "approximately 1745 hours Rocky Mountain time."

After only about 90 seconds the tech reported back. "I've found three keyhole satellites that had coverage of that area at that time. Hold one."

As Mark waited he visualized the computer renditions that the tech was seeing and conveying the coverage of the three satellite inputs. While they would not get a horizontal view of the chopper they would get a 30 to 40 degree lateral shot depending on the location of the satellites at the time.

The tech came back, "Sir, I have four Helios in that vicinity at that time. Can you clarify the target?"

Mark smiled, "Disregard the USAF Apache AH-64, the CBI platform, and the Channel 2 news chopper and see if you can get me an ID on the other one."

The tech deleted the first three choppers and triangulated on the fourth one. "Sir, the highest of the choppers is at approximately 2800 feet from ground level, it is a Bell 439 corporate model. Hold one."

Again it was less than a minute when the tech came back with more information. "General, that chopper is a 439 and it is registered to the Holt Corporation, based out of Reno, Nevada."

Mark wrote the information down. "Can you get me an ID on the occupants?"

After another "Hold one" and a longer wait the tech chuckled, "Sir, you're not going to believe this but we got two positives. I've got one on the pilot and one on the man sitting in the other front seat. The pilot is Gene Gutterman, the registered pilot for the Holt Corporation for that aircraft. The other man is a high level enforcer for the mob in Nevada. His name is George Teller. I'm sure there is an interesting story as to why he is in a Holt Corp helio over a running gun battle in Colorado."

Mark laughed, "Son, fax me all the information you have on George Teller and then run that video to its conclusion and you'll see something else interesting." He gave the tech Jack's fax number and then hung up.

While they waited for the fax, Jack asked Mark what the tech meant when he said there could be an interesting story about Teller on that helicopter.

Mark was thinking about what they had learned. "Huh? Oh yeah. The Holt Corporation is one of the top military re-fitters for Air Force, Army, and Navy aircraft. They are squeaky clean and the government makes sure that they stay that way. What a mobster is doing in one of their aircraft with their pilot would raise a lot of eyebrows and definitely take a great deal of explaining to protect their contracts if the information got out. And, I'm sure the proper people will be investigating this seeming inconsistency."

Jack asked Mark, "Well, do we go after the mobster and his connections or do we work on the Holt Corporation?"

The fax machine chimed to notify receipt of incoming data. Mark walked over and picked up the fax sheets, one of which was a photo. Staring at the picture he nodded.

Mark looked at the assembled people. "I say, let's work the mobster angle on all of our levels. Carol, you see what the CBI and FBI have on this character. Sensei, you see what you can unearth through the police and Interpol. Honey, you see what the Mossad can add and I will see what the NSA and CIA have that they will give us."

Jack, Laura, and Minister Throman decided to inquire of the Lord concerning the spiritual connection between the mobster and the demonic events leading up to today.

CHAPTER THIRTY

Twelve hours later the same group re-gathered in the living room of Castle Malone. Mark had them give their summaries one at a time.

Carol Nolan came up with better photos of George Teller and some tracking data but not much from the CBI. The FBI had a good sized file on Teller and gave some of it to Carol as a courtesy but they kept the really important data to themselves due to an ongoing investigation into the mob. That information included known associates, whereabouts, and recent activities.

Sensei Grady had considerable information from Interpol concerning the supposed activities of George Teller on the international arms market but no substantial proof. The local police had almost nothing on him but a name and a warning as to his 'connections'.

Sarah's contacts with her old employer netted major Intel. George Teller himself was a minor nobody in the current situation. He was an organizer and a planner. He was obviously not overly competent considering the failed attempts on the team members. The Mossad took a different angle and dug into his finances and associates. They had unearthed a shadowy connection that might be financing his activities to acquire the crucifixion nail.

Sarah shook her head. "I had no idea people like this existed in the modern world. But, it seems that there is an organization, based in Jordan that espouses the belief in first century Canaanite gods. They are called the "Neo-Idealist League" or NIL but I would call them the neo-idolists. The trouble they have stirred up has been selective but vicious. They are somewhat protected by, but not approved by the Jordanian government. The Mossad has watched them for several years now and they were simply a bothering gnat that you'd like to swat but isn't worth the trouble."

She took a drink of the water from her glass. "About the time Jack acquired the crucifixion nail the NIL suddenly came into great wealth. The Mossad are not sure of the source of these funds but estimates them to be in the upper range of seven hundred million dollars, U.S. They have begun to support various terrorists groups on a selective basis. Again, we don't know why. David Zahavy believes that this group bankrolled your original enemy, Don Miland. They also believe that it was their money that supported the Omniscience Temple until your efforts led to it being hunted out of existence."

Sarah looked to her husband. "Mark and I want to research these nutcases and see if they aren't the money and brains behind all these attacks. If they are, then we need to figure out how to eliminate the entire operation."

As Sarah sat down, Mark rose and continued the conversation. "After going over the Intel and the new NAS and CIA information concerning this group I think the conclusion will be that they are the front organization for the devil's push to get the nail. These are the elusive "masterminds" behind every effort to date to get the treasure for the Lord of Darkness."

Mark used the terms he knew that Jack and Laura would use but wasn't completely comfortable yet talking about spiritual powers.

"We need to be very careful that they don't know that we've tumbled to them or they will disappear. The Intel supports the concept that they were behind Don Miland, hence the drive to get all of you as a result of your involvement. They weren't apparently involved with Max Lister and Muammar Qaddafi in that Children's Ranch thing or the Tel Aviv and United States poison attacks. They were backers of the Omniscience Templethough, and I wonder why they don't include Stan and Debby Hargrove" These were the ex-Salt Lake City Police Captain and his wife who helped them defeat the Master Prophets of the Omniscience Temple and then became employees of Mark's company.

Mark gestured, pointing to the east, "I believe that these guys are the source of all the evil that has been happening to you, and us." He stopped and stared at Jack.

Jack smiled. "You might be right about this particular bunch, but remember, the real enemy is Satan. He is working through this group and we do need to see that they are stopped permanently. Unfortunately that will probably end the battle but not the war. You know the burden the nail has placed on all of us. I think we need to take our concept of this war to the next level. We need to realize that we will simply be eliminating the cancer and not the cause of the cancer. Only Yahshua will be able to stop Satan from causing us grief. Until he comes back and locks that old snake up for a thousand years as it describes in Revelation, we need to stand up to everything he can try to do to us."

Jack looked at the assembled cast, "That means every one of you could be a target until the day you die. So, I, for one, am going to get used to it, see it for what it is, the frantic attempts of an already defeated foe to cause Yahveh trouble. I didn't pick this role, but I can assure you that none of you did either. Yahveh selected each of us to bear our part in this burden. And I believe He will depend on us to keep the nail safe and out of the enemy's hands. Consider this a lifetime "mission" for the Lord."

Jack asked the Minister to add his part to the meeting.

Alan Throman looked anything but like a hero. An elderly man, with wispy white hair, what there was left of it, and a small frame. Nevertheless, he was spry for a man near his eighties and had a very agile mind which saw to the root of a problem, especially one concerning spiritual matters.

Alan stood and smiled at everyone in the group. He had come to know each and every one and could honestly say that he loved them and had the highest regard for their abilities and their callings. "What the Lord revealed to Jack, Laura, and I when we sought Him in prayer was extremely interesting. I won't bother you with the individual visions, or dreams, but just relate the revelation and the interpretations we sought for these communications from above. It seems at present that three forces are being "led" by the enemy against our group. The first is a terrible group that Yahveh is about to destroy for their rebellion and hatred for Him. I now believe that group is this NIL you're talking about."

Alan started pacing back and forth."The second prong of the enemy's attack is directly spiritual but carried out in the physical world. Demons that can access our dimension directly are attempting to secure the nail for their master by their own actions rather than relying on people."

Jack spoke up. "You mean the large man who came out of and went back into the ground and the black cloud on the mountain property?"

Alan nodded. "Yes, yes. Both of those and others you haven't seen, at least not yet. They represent the urgency the Prince of the Power of the Air is feeling to secure the nail. Most people feel that spirits can't interact with the physical world. They're wrong. You have seen several cases of proof now with your own eyes. Now the third prong of his attack is harder to understand, but it seems that it may be possible that someone on the inside of our group is going to, let us say, unknowingly, aid and abet the enemy in their efforts to secure the nail by deception. I believe that this person will be tempted by something almost beyond their will to resist regardless of the costs. I would like to remind everyone that all gifts of Satan contain a "seed" of death in them. They always look inviting and wonderful at first but sooner or later they will turn to dross and the sin involved will be very destructive."

That statement made everyone look around to see if they could determine who might be the weak link. Everyone that was, except Jack who looked at the minister and said, "I think I will be the one that you're talking about."

Mark's face clouded over, "NO WAY! No way you are about to help Satan get the nail. I don't think so!"

Jack's lop-sided smile was an acknowledgment of Mark's friendship and belief in him. "Thanks buddy, but don't you see? I'm the only one that really has access to the nail. Who else would the enemy be able to use?"

Laura laughed, "Don't forget me. I can access the treasure too."

Alan held up his hands, stopping the conversation. "No, Jack it probably is not you nor Laura. It may be none of you. This is a possibility only. We just need to watch ourselves and check anything we do against the word of Yahveh. Have others check any time you get an urge to do something that doesn't match up to our game plan. This possibility could have been planted in our minds by the enemy to destroy our unity. Keep your faith in the Lord Yahshua and we will overcome any attempts to beat us."

As everyone relaxed and fell silent, Mark stood to his feet. "Okay folks. The major problem confronting us concerning the NIL is that they are a close knit group of Islamic radicals who know each other. We will never be able to put an informer in their ranks because of that familiarity. So," He tilted his head at his wife. "The lady spy and I have worked out a high-tech attack that stands a good chance of working. I will show it to you tomorrow, if all the parts come in, and, if everything works." He ground to a halt and smiled a hopeful smile.

Jack suggested everyone get their lives in order to allow for a short stay outside the U.S.

After everyone dispersed Jack told Mark, "I think we need the services of Gary Eisenthal. This "second prong" attack on the physical/spiritual planes needs the help of someone who's mastered in spiritual warfare and I can't think of anyone better than Gary."

Mark grinned. "Yeah, but do you think he'll be up for another round with us? The last time it almost got him killed."

Jack shrugged, "All we can do is ask."

CHAPTER THIRTY-ONE

Gary Eisenthal was reaching the end of his patience. The two women that had come to his office were once again debating between themselves the possibility of Christians having demons.

Gary had delivered hundreds of people, primarily Christians, quietly and simply by praying to Yahshua and determining the root cause of the infestation. They only rarely interfaced with demons because it was risky, usually unproductive, and it gave them power because you focus on them. He never talked to demons if the Holy Spirit didn't lead him to do it. He knew better than to assume authority where he didn't have any. Of course then, he didn't even charge for his services because he had been given the task by the Lord.

But, if these two women didn't stop wasting his time he was going to cause both of them to need additional deliverance.

As they started on round twenty-nine of their unchanging positions, Gary pushed the button on his intercom and then slapped his hand on the desk in front of him. "Enough!" He spoke into the intercom. "Mandy, would you come in here please." Then he looked at the two women. "Sister Lammer, please go out into my waiting room and stay there while I work with Sister Markas."

The women looked at each other. Sister Lammer got up and walked out of the room. Sister Markas stared at Gary with concern. Mandy walked into the office and closed the door to the waiting room.

Gary made it a point to never work alone with a member of the opposite sex to prevent damage to either one of their reputations. This was standard Christian counseling practice and it made good sense.

Thirty minutes later, a newly energized, gratefully free, and much happier Sister Markas left in the company of a mildly confused Sister Lammer.

Mandy looked at her boss. "Do you think Mrs. Lammer will want deliverance?"

Gary smiled, "I think that her friend's deliverance will convince her that she could really use the same. Mrs. Markas grew up with a sexually abusive father and the loss of innocence, not to mention shame and guilt and the loss of the safety in her home almost totally destroyed her self-image as a young woman. She found a husband that loved her, contrary to the trend of most abused women who tend to replace the "bad" relative with an equally "bad" mate. This gave her the ability to function somewhat in society but she was plagued by thoughts of lust and suicide. Her husband knew of my services through their church and he got her to come here. She brought her friend as protection. Now she's smiling and loves Yahveh so much it'll shine through to her questioning friend."

The phone rang and Mandy answered it. She listened and then handed it to Gary. "Who's Mark Connelly? And what is a Sand Snake?"

Gary smiled and took the phone. "Mr. Connelly. How are you? How is the rest of your crew doing?"

After listening for a few minutes he nodded and hung up. "Mandy, can we rearrange my schedule for the next few weeks?"

Mandy looked at her calendar, "Sure if you don't mind missing the convention you were planning to be at in Seattle."

Gary thought about the convention and Mark's offer. Some people talk about things, others do something about them. Gary was a doer, not a talker. "Cancel the conference and rearrange my schedule. Then take a well-earned two week paid vacation."

The amount of money Mark offered him would cover his whole year including Mandy's vacation. Gary thought, "Of course, this may take longer than two weeks and I'll have to extend her vacation. On the other hand I would get more money if it takes longer. He remembered the Israeli desert late at night and realized that he could face dangers he would never have to face normally. Great!" He packed quickly and headed for the airport in Los Angeles to catch the flight that Mark had reserved for him.

CHAPTER THIRTY-TWO

As Gary Eisenthal reclined in the first-class seat on the Boeing 767 for the flight to Denver he thought back to another case that had shown him that, while Yahveh is all-powerful, people aren't.

-------------------------******-------------------------

Four years before, he had been asked by a major television evangelist for help with a particularly bothersome spiritual problem. Gary had flown to Maryland to the impressive headquarters of the international ministry and talked to several people including the evangelist himself concerning this manifestation. It seems that this particular spirit was disrupting the meetings, causing concern, and even attempting to reverse healings done by the Lord at recent conventions.

Gary was able to determine that all the intercessory prayers, rebuking, and pre-meeting prayer coverage was in place each time but apparently didn't do anything to deter this evil spirit. To Gary this meant that the spirit had legal right to be where he had appeared.

Going over their records, Gary was able to determine the presence of only six individuals whose presence coincided for with all six of the sightings. He was able to eliminate four of them immediately by talking to them and letting Yahveh's Holy Spirit lead him in making these determinations.

That left only two people who could have been the doorway for this evil spirit's access to the meetings. One was the evangelist himself and the other was his music director. Gary knew in his heart that the evangelist was too much in love with Yahshua to walk in sin and not seek forgiveness and repentance. That only left the music director who had been present at each appearance of this demon. There was no time for Gary to check his hypothesis by leaving the music director behind on one trip to see if the spirit appeared or not. He had to determine the validity of his theory some other way.

As he sought Yahveh in prayer about the problem he noticed a sort of flickering of his vision. He suddenly went cold all over and his vision faded out until he could see nothing at all. His hearing centered on the harsh, heavy breathing which sounded like it was right next to his head. Something clammy and very hot seemed to slide through his chest and clutch his very heart. Trying to speak did not produce any sounds he could hear but Gary had been in similar situations a couple of times. He knew demons could mess with his hearing but could not stop his mental voice. Especially with the words he was thinking/speaking. "My sovereign Master Yahshua, I ask you to have your mighty angels restrain this spirit who is trespassing by attacking me. I am your follower and as you said to Saul on the road to Damascus, "Saul, Saul, why are you persecuting me?" when he thought he was only persecuting the followers of the way he was actually persecuting the Master of the Universe. So, spirit, you are now trespassing against Yahshua himself!"

Suddenly his sight and hearing returned, the cold and hot feelings, and the chest problems disappeared completely. But Gary wasn't finished with this character. "Holy Spirit of Yahveh, reveal to me the name of this evil spirit that attacked this child of the Master Yahshua."

Gary clearly heard, "Pride".

"This is the music director you are referring to I assume?"

No, it is the evangelist. He thinks he is Yahveh's chosen one and much smarter than ordinary men."

Gary was in shock, but he thought, "Holy Spirit, is this the truth?"

He was assured that it was the truth.

Gary prayed, "What do I do to break this spirit of pride's hold on him?"

The direction he got was to face the evangelist with the problem and have the evangelist pray for forgiveness and repentance.

Gary asked the Holy Spirit to take the evil spirit to the pit as he made his way to the room that the evangelist was staying in. He asked the two security guards that were outside the door for permission for a short visit with the man. They checked and ushered him into the room and then left the two men alone. The evangelist was eager to hear what Gary had uncovered.

Gary was going to slowly approach the subject and test the waters carefully, but before he could formulate the first word, a condemnation, of which he was not the author, rolled out of his mouth. He could only listen in awe to what his voice was saying.

"Beware!" Gary said to the dark-haired evangelist. "Let me tell you what the Son of Yahveh says to you."

"Tell me," the man replied.

Gary said, "Although you were once small in your own eyes, did you not become the head of an internationally acclaimed ministry? I, your Elohim, anointed you and sent you on a mission, saying, `Go and heal the sick in My Name. Why did you open the door to sin? Yahshua says, "I saw Satan fall like lightning from heaven. I have given you authority to preach good news, heal the sick and to overcome all the power of the enemy. I told you nothing will harm you. However, you have allowed pride to enter your heart and with it idol worship. You worship yourself and your abilities and are in danger of Satan's fate. Repent NOW and ask for my forgiveness or in My anger you will never be with me!"

Gary sat there and watched the face of the evangelist as it displayed the emotions of shock, understanding of his sin, and utter dismay. He dropped to his knees and began to cry out to Yahveh for forgiveness of his pride, foolishness, and even his culpability in allowing the evil one to turn his head and his heart from worshiping Yahveh. His repentance was true and from the heart. He had been completely deceived into thinking he was doing everything for Yahveh when it had slowly but carefully skewed into being able to do it because he was so good. Gary sat there transfixed by the man as he poured out his heart and sought forgiveness to the Savior he truly loved.

Suddenly Gary was startled as he spoke again. "Your earnest plea has been heard and forgiveness will be yours but you shall carry a reminder in your body from now on, to focus your thoughts and worship only on Yahveh." As these words were spoken, the evangelist grabbed his right hip and let out a small moan. From that day on he always walked with a slight limp. But his smile was framed by his tears of thankfulness.

Gary had flown back home after that episode with a new respect for how the mighty can fall, and not even know they were falling. The enemy's ability to twist a ministry or a talent into an idol was subtle and effective.

----------------------✱✱✱✱✱----------------------

As the big jet winged its way to Denver and a new adventure, Gary fell asleep knowing that he too had to be on his guard. This time, against his own pride.

CHAPTER THIRTY-THREE

As Gary Eisenthal sat back in the rear seat of the limo taking him into South Denver he relaxed and watched the scenery flow by soundlessly on the other side of the glass. He had been to Denver many times and always liked the town. He was mentally relaxing prior to his meeting with Mark and Jack and learning what they were up against this time, when he had a vision. This surprised Gary because he knew about other people's visions but had never had one of his own.

He stood next to a small child in a dark and foreboding ancient city. The sky was black with the dark of a stormy night and he was filled with an indefinable fear. He noticed that there were thousands or millions of other children of all nationalities around him, most of them babies or newborns lying on the rocky ground. There were modern national flags on staffs scattered around with the children. He saw the flag of the United States of America with what seemed to be millions of small bodies around it. He didn't see another adult anywhere.

There was a commotion to his left which resolved itself into a rising volume of cries and screams. He turned to the left and saw a wall of fire moving his way and consuming all the children as it came. The children were packed so tightly they couldn't get away from the fire as it came to them. They cried out as they were engulfed in it and then were stilled. The fire was almost to him... The vision faded out and was replaced by the quiet flow of the Denver suburbs outside the limo.

Gary noticed that he was sweating and he could still feel the heat generated by the fire in the vision on his left side. His whole body was shaking and he prayed. "Father Yahveh, Why did I receive that vision? Was it a warning?"

He clearly heard a single word. "Molech"

As he sat there he thought about the meaning of the name Molech or Moloch; an Old Testament Canaanite god of fire to whom children were offered in sacrifice. He is also known as an Assyrian god. Molech was mentioned as early as the 3rd millennium BC, although most known references to him come from the later period represented by the Hebrew Bible. In which, Solomon and later Ahaz introduced the worship of this detestable deity into Judah. He had a sanctuary at Topheth, in the valley of Hinnom south of Jerusalem.

Gary thought back to his history lessons. On the west and southwest side of Jerusalem is a valley which was called in the Bible, the Valley of Ben Hinnom. One area in this valley was named Topheth which meant altar. Topheth and the Valley of Ben Hinnom were used as a garbage dump, and a place where the bodies of executed criminals were disposed of. A continual fire was kept burning to dispose of the refuse deposited there. It was truly a contemptible, hellish place. The Greek word for hell, gehenna, was a transliteration from the Hebrew ge-hinnom (the Valley of Hinnom). Also, in Isaiah 30:33, Topheth is spoken of as a place of punishment and burning that the Messiah has been preparing for evil people and will Himself ignite.

Topheth was the place where children were killed during pagan rituals as sacrifices to Molech, "the detestable god of the Ammonites." The sacrifice of children profanes the name of Yahveh because it is the savage destruction of completely innocent creatures that bear His likeness. It is an act of sedition against the throne of Yahveh, an act that demonstrates utmost contempt for what Yahveh values very highly. The sacrifice of children is at its very root an insurrection against the authority of Yahveh. Those who spill the blood of children are repeating the infamous words "Who is the Master Yahshua, that I should obey His voice?" The sacrifice of children is also an act of devotion to demons who have established themselves as competitors to the true Yahveh. Gary remembered Psalms 106:37-38 in the New International Version of the Bible which states, "They sacrificed their sons and their daughters to demons. They shed innocent blood, the blood of their sons and daughters, whom they sacrificed to the idols of Canaan, and the land was desecrated by their blood."

Gary thought about the vision he had had. It was obviously a reference to both the similar practices of modern day abortion and the ancient "passing children through the wall of fire" that the followers of Molech did to their children. He thought about the vision and the "wall of fire" that was destroying the children.

Gary was sure the demon Molech was still around today. Today Molech still deceives people into sacrificing their children to him and goes by various names around the world as causes that purport to cater to women's health. Gary knew that Yahveh is saddened at what occurs at those places; The Lord describes abortion as detestable and unthinkable. Gary thought of the passage in Jeremiah, 32:35 in the NIV. "They built high places for Ba'al in the Valley of Ben Hinnom to sacrifice their sons and daughters to Molech, though I never commanded, nor did it enter my mind, that they should do such a detestable thing."

Gary was sure that the Master Yahshua was appalled by the routine and unremitting human slaughter at Topheth. The killing of little children was sanctioned and encouraged by the governing authority. King Manasseh, who began to rule in 696 B.C., Today abortion is the modern equivalent of the worship of Molech and the governing authorities are still approving the carnage.

As the limo left the highway and turned off the frontage road into a gated community, Gary wondered how his vision and the demon Molech was involved in what he was about to become a part of in a few minutes. One thing was for sure, it was definitely involved. Yahveh's Holy Spirit didn't send irrelevant messages.

The limo drew up the circular drive to a beautiful but somewhat odd building for a residential neighborhood. It had no windows. That didn't detract from the graceful lines of the house but seemed, strange.

Gary slid out of the back seat as the door was opened by the driver. He walked up the stairs to the front entrance and pushed the button that was apparently the door bell. A minute later the door was opened by Jack Malone who grinned and hugged Gary and brought him and his luggage into the house.

Gary was glad to meet Laura, Mark, and Sarah again and there were heartfelt greetings all around. They adjourned to the living room and the foursome listened as Gary brought them up to date on his doings over the last year since they had traveled the sands of the desert together in the Israeli "Sand Snake" and faced down a demonic presence at the risk of their lives.

Mark then brought him up to date on the new problem. As he listened to the attacks and investigations that had led them to the Middle East country of Jordan he realized that the Holy Spirit's vision dovetailed perfectly into their quest. He waited until Mark was finished and then told them of his vision.

Laura was horrified by the descriptions of children being destroyed by fire. She asked Gary how that vision was a part of what they were attempting to resolve with the NIL in Jordan.

Gary composed his thoughts and started explaining his idea. I've heard about this NIL. There is a demon, named Astrophel involved in this terrorist organization. As I understand it, this demon has a direct relationship to the original demon that possessed Herod the Great in Yahshua's day. These people in the NIL have adopted Herod's concept that destruction of all the enemy's children will let them dominate the world. Now understand, these people are also Muslim extremists. So, the "enemy" in this case is the infidels. An infidel is anyone who isn't a Muslim and I think in this case, anyone who isn't a Muslim extremist with views identical to their own.

The entire operation is saturated with demonic influences which possess every one at a base they have in Jordan. The demonic force is ranging around that area and has, virtually, full control of anyone who is involved in their terrorist activities." He was about to continue when the door chime interrupted him.

Jack flipped on the TV and selected the front door camera. One of the two men standing in the front portico at their door was very familiar. Sarah jumped up and ran to the door. Opening it up she grabbed the dapper man in a bear hug and laughed. "David Zahavy, what are you doing here in Denver?"

The Mossad leader hugged her back and shrugged, "Since I was in the neighborhood I thought that I'd drop by." He stepped back and gestured to the tall thin man next to him, "Sarah, I would like you to meet a friend of mine, Ariel Tzvi. He is one of the best Jewish experts on terrorism and Muslim extremists. I presume that your team is about to embark on a quest into our part of the world and possibly to get involved with one of our enemies. This is not a good thing... unless you invite me along to show you all the sights." Sarah smiled a heartfelt welcome and laughed at her old friend's nonchalant attitude about such dangerous matters. She invited them in and shut the door behind them. She then showed them into the living room.

Greetings were made as the newcomer was welcomed to Castle Malone. David looked around and smiled. "You will have to show me the secret of this window that is not a window. This would be very welcome in Israel."

Jack shrugged, "The secret is for sale but since it is you, maybe we can work a deal." David walked over and looked closely at the image portrayed on the "window". He felt a presence and found Gary standing right next to him with a surprised look on his face. Gary shook his head. "I felt there was something funny as I drove up and didn't see any windows on the house. But, I really didn't notice that there were windows on the inside until you said something. That is really something!"

Jack sobered up and told both men that he would show them the window operation after they had a chance to discuss the matters at hand. Everyone sat down in the comfortable sofas and chairs arranged in the conversational circle. Jack and Mark updated everyone on their recent experiences. David gave them a short update on things he had been doing since they had left Israel over a year ago. But not everything, after all the Mossad still has to keep some secrets.

After David and Ari had heard about the attacks and Gary's vision, David held up his hand. "I have been working on the requests that Sarah made through me, which it turned out concerned the NIL and their base in Jordan." He reached into his jacket and brought out a piece of paper he unfolded and turned so everyone else could see it. It was a map of the Jordanian nation and had the NIL location marked. "You can see that they are located 55 miles south-southwest of Blair and approximately 40 miles north-northwest of Al Jafe in the deep Jordanian desert. They picked this extremely remote location so that they can detect anyone attempting to approach their base. The enormous amount of money they have received in the last few years has allowed them to buy and install the latest in high-tech security equipment. They even have their own satellite that maintains a geo-synchronous orbit and has excellent daytime vision and even better nighttime infrared cameras. The Intel intercept capabilities of the satellite are the best that the Germans who built the satellite could provide".

He looked at everyone there. "Please realize that we believe that these people have a much more extensive underground facility at this location than you can see from the air. We do know that they are fanatics that will kill anybody that tries to interfere with their operations. They have surrounded their facility with a nomadic tribe of Muslim extremists. These people are very competent in desert warfare and know the vicinity of the facility like their own back yard. They tolerate nobody to cross their enclave which is about ten miles deep unless authorized by the NIL. Since all movement of the NIL seems to be by VTL aircraft they don't have to worry about guests. We have lost two operatives to this group in the last month." David made a small face with pursed lips. "Of course, we paid them back several times over, but it still hurts that these desert tribesmen are professional enough to detect and intercept our people.

The reason that I am here is that the Mossad wants to get a handle on what they are doing as badly as you do, maybe even worse. There have been rumors lately that they are working on a way to destroy children the world over. But I digress. You see, the problem you are suffering with is only a small part of the overall NIL game plan. They are into soft terrorism in a major way. Such as the abortion movements all over the world, many of which are supported by NIL money and, if necessary, personnel such as doctors. We believe that they are one of the world's largest and most effective backers of hard terrorism against the western world and of course Israel. The Jordanian government looks the other way." David shook his head and looked at Mark and Jack, "Something both our governments know all about, plausible deniability."

Mark was listening to everything the Mossad leader said with great interest. He jumped in at that point. "Okay, it is obvious that this NIL group is a much bigger fish than we supposed. But, if that is the case, why are they bankrolling the attacks on us, which must be only a small line item on their agenda?"

Ari replied. "Because the Christian artifact you call the crucifixion nail has, mistakenly in my view, become the crux of their world."

That got everyone's attention. The tall man continued, "Please, understand that I am Jewish. I personally don't believe in Yahshua or that he was the Messiah. I really don't understand why this artifact has any bearing on the NIL or the Muslim world. But, my understanding aside, apparently the entire future for the NIL seems to be hinged on acquiring that ancient artifact." Ari rolled his eyes in disbelief.

He continued, "David's people were able to "persuade" one of the NIL people to explain some things about how they operate. This was two days ago. The evidence of what they are attempting to do was verifiable. Once I saw the connection, I went to David and we came directly here. Your nail, again for reasons I personally don't understand, is probably the most important asset in this group of terrorist's world. The enemy of Yahveh also apparently places great importance on acquiring the crucifixion nail. He has instructed many others like the NIL, who do the devil's work in this world, to acquire it. Let me explain how that nail, which survived for the last 2000 years, has become so critical to these people. There is an eighteen hundred year-old prophesy in the Arab world that goes something like this:

"Your world is balanced on one of three daggers. Possess it and you will ascend to the heights,

lose it and you will fall. If you ascend, the morning crops of your enemies can be destroyed. If you fall, you will be destroyed. The morning star cannot rise without the last dagger. The last dagger represents life or death.

The interpretation of this prophesy has changed many times over the years but the NIL strangely now believes it finally understands this prophesy properly. Their interpretation is that their world of terror hinges on the single remaining crucifixion nail out of the three that were used to pin your messiah to the cross at Golgotha. If they can acquire it, then they will be able to destroy the infidels. If they can't get it then they will not succeed. The reference to the "morning crops of your enemies" we believe means non-Muslim children. So, if they believe if they can get the nail then they can destroy the children of their enemies throughout the world. If they can't get it, then they will be destroyed instead. The comment that the "morning star" can't rise without the nail refers to Satan. Apparently he has attached great value to it and is desperately seeking it. It is probably the conclusion of too many Arabs smoking too many funny cigarettes, but that is what is happening." Ari looked at them for comments.

Laura asked him, "But if it is that critical to Satan and all these terrorists groups, why has there has been such ineffectual efforts against us? I would think that they would throw everything they have at us to get the nail. I doubt that we could withstand the massive attacks they could mount.

Ari held up his hand for attention. "The reason that they haven't brought all their guns to bear on you is threefold. First, because they have other, even more pressing problems they have to handle along with finding this nail. Remember, this prophesy is over eighteen hundred years old and the interpretations tend to be inaccurate and are not always sure or respected. Second, they are not sure that the nail you are supposed to have is the "third dagger" that they seek."

David spoke up. "What you probably haven't heard is that they have carried out similar raids on over a dozen different possible "nail" holders around the world. In other words, they aren't sure if you are the real target, yet."

Ari continued, "Thirdly, David believes that Yahveh is on your side and He is making it hard for them to get a good shot at you. You know, for them it is sort of like trying to pick up a heavy ball bearing set so that you can only get a grip on the top half of the ball bearing. It is also coated with really slippery oil. Every time they move in your direction, Yahveh confuses them or deflects their efforts. David also feels that Yahveh will continue to do this while you work out a solution to the problem. I can assure you that the problem of the nail is not black and white or cut and dried for the enemy. They can only assume that you have the real one of what they seek. However, if they ever are convinced that you hold the "third dagger" you will have a serious problem." Ari finished and sat down.

David added, "They have already begun to look more in your direction because of the lack of success of their teams in your case."

Jack asked David, "What is their success rate with the other raids?"

David frowned somewhat, "One hundred percent success at proving those people don't have the third dagger. But, these terrorists are thorough and they have left no survivors either. You aren't their only remaining possibility but the field is rapidly narrowing and after three botched attempts they are beginning to see a heavenly involvement in your case. This support from Yahveh could be the thing that points them completely in your direction before long."

Laura shook her head, "What do we do? We can't destroy the nail, and we can't give it to someone else who could lose it. If they concentrate on us then sooner or later we are going to lose somebody and have to decide between them and the nail. I don't know if I could do it if it was any of you." She looked around the room and sighed.

David pursed his lips, "I know better than to offer the services of the Mossad to protect the crucifixion nail for all the obvious reasons. That plus the fact that I know Yahveh gave it to Jack to protect. I have to assume that

He knows what He is doing and we have to stand our ground regardless of the pressure."

Ari just shook his head.

It had gotten dark and after a catered-in supper and three more hours of discussion, Laura and Jack put everyone in their rooms and got ready for bed. Laura pulled the cover up and snuggled into Jack's shoulder. He put his arm around her and held her close. She asked quietly, "What do we do?"

Jack thought for a second and said, "Let's pray."

CHAPTER THIRTY-FOUR

Jack and Laura prayed for a while and then rested in the Lord to see what the Lord would give them as an answer to their prayers. Laura fell halfway asleep and was not surprised when she found herself standing on a cliff overlooking the ocean. As before, the ocean view was magnificent, the sun softly warm, and the breeze delightful. She turned around and found Rose watching her from a short distance away. In her dream Laura walked over to the angel and smiled. "How are you Rose?"

The angel returned the smile, "I'm fine Laura, and how are you holding up?"

"I don't know how well I'm doing this time. It seems we may have gotten ourselves directly into the crosshairs of Satan and his people. I am worried about my husband and our friends." Laura knew she wasn't being very brave but she wanted to speak the truth, even if it wasn't the proper thing to say to the angel.

Rose seemed to sit down in mid-air and studied Laura for a minute. "You are concerned aren't you? Well, know this, that Yahveh is not the author of fear, worry, or disorder. None of you will solve this problem with your skill, intelligence, or bravery. It is by the power of the Holy Spirit of Yahveh you will succeed, not through a man or woman's abilities."

Laura nodded her head, "Of course. Jack and I just really want to follow Yahveh's direction in this matter."

The angel seemed to look inwardly for a few seconds. "What if Yahveh's direction places you and those you love in harm's way? Would your faith rise up and enable you to say "yes" to Yahveh's will if it could lose you your husband?"

Laura was taken aback. This was the first time she'd heard Rose talk like this, especially in mentioning the end of life for her or Jack. She thought about it for a few seconds and then gave her concerns to the Lord. "Jack and I are committed to follow your will Father Yahveh, regardless of the situations or potential losses.

We both have given our lives to you, Yahshua and we know that Your will is our best choice regardless of the results. Out loud she said to Rose, "Yes, I would follow the Lord's will if it meant I could die, or lose the man I love more than my life."

Rose nodded, "Then, you have just answered your own question." Rose started to fade from sight. A last comment came softly, "Remember, the best defense is usually a good offense."

Laura woke up to find Jack sitting up in bed watching her. "What?"

Jack was very serious, more serious with her than she could ever remember. "Did you know you talk out loud when you run into angels in your sleep?"

She thought about her conversation with Rose and how her side of it would sound. She reached out and hugged Jack fiercely, "I'm sorry if it sounded callous but I was telling her the truth."

Jack continued to hold her and did not reply. This was the first time he really realized that he could lose Laura. It had never bothered him to put himself in jeopardy but now it was both of them on the front line. He was sure that Yahveh would take care of either of them if the other was called home to heaven but it unsettled him anyway.

Eventually he released her and held her at arms length in the dim light of the bedroom. "Laura, I love you so much. I know that Yahveh will take care of either of us regardless what happens to the other person. But, I would be lost without you and I just... "

Laura hushed him, "I know how much you love me and I love you just as much. This life is only temporary and the better one is for the rest of eternity. We will be together then too. I would never have dreamed that I would have been involved in all the things we've done in the last two years. But, I would not have missed being by your side for anything. I'm learning that to enjoy life you need to experience it. I've become an action-adventure junkie for Yahveh. I would give my life up for you in a New York second and I know you would do the same for me. For you and I, we now have to live the twenty-third psalm, "Yea, though we walk through the valley of shadow of death, we shall fear no evil, because our Lord is with us."

Jack felt the tears falling from her eyes and he kissed them away. "All right, what did Rose tell you?"

Laura snuffled, sighed, and blew her nose. Then she summed it up, "The best defense is usually a good offense!"

Jack said, "I see." He looked at the large blue-green readout in the wall. It showed 2:40 AM. "Let's try to get some sleep and tackle this tomorrow."

Laura agreed, "Jack, I want you to know that Castle Malone makes me feel safe, being with you makes me feel safer, and being with Yahshua the safest of all. I just want you to know that I appreciate everything."

He kissed her good night and fell to sleep considering their options.

He soon found himself walking through a fog or a mist that was getting brighter. Out of the mist came a man in all black and he radiated evil. Jack rebuked him in the name of the Lord Yahshua of Nazareth who came in the flesh, and then asked Yahveh's Holy Spirit to bind the man in black. Jack then deflected the waves of fear that the demon was trying to impress on him by quoting 2Timothy verse 7 - *For Yahveh hath not given us the spirit of fear; but of power, and of love, and of a sound mind.*

Jack then prayed that Yahshua would have two of his warrior angels torment this spirit until he told Jack the truth why he was trespassing against Yahshua.

The words Jack heard were not spoken but simply heard in his mind. "I am come to torment you and to divide you and your friends. My master knows you are coming against him and he is moving all hell to stop you." Even though the spirit man was bound by the Holy Spirit of God, he radiated confidence in his determination. There was a darkness surrounding him that grew slowly in size and depth. Jack wasn't sure of his next step and was considering having the angels dispatch this spirit to the pit when he noticed a definite growing light to his right.

As he looked he saw Caleb walking towards them. He was holding a flaming sword at guard position with both hands. The confidence and darkness surrounding the demon dwindled quickly as Caleb walked past Jack and spoke to the evil spirit, At this point, the darkness fled from the light surrounding Caleb. "You foul essence; you have been convicted of trespassing against the Son of Yahveh. I am here in the name of the Lord Yahshua to execute your sentence. With one mighty swing the sword cut the spirit man in half. Both halves dissolved into smoke and dissipated into the mist. Caleb sheathed his sword and turned to Jack. "The best thing to do with their type is to destroy them. Don't talk to them, just burn them up in the fire of the Most High's Holy Spirit or cast them into the lake of fire."

Jack added, "Or to call upon a mighty angel with a sword of fire."

Caleb came closer to Jack. "I have a word for you from the Lord. "*These people who are attacking you are an abomination in My sight. Go up against them and I will give them into your hand. Give ear to my commandments, utterly destroy all that they are and have, and spare them not; but slay both man and woman, and completely destroy any devices, creations, or efforts they have made. Do all that I say because their evil is beyond belief and will corrupt even the Saints if it endures*".

Caleb felt the stricken feeling in Jack's heart. "Do not be faint of heart concerning these commandments. There is not one that can be saved of this group. They are about to unleash a power into the air over all of their enemy's lands that they believe will destroy all children from newborn to those coming of age. But the evil one who drives these people knows that it will change in a short time to destroy all young life on the planet, including the terrorist's. Yahveh does not want that to happen and you are his chosen weapon to prevent it. And prevent it you must."

Caleb smiled at Jack in his dream. The Lord will be with you and your friends." He turned and began to walk away. Jack saw him put his hand on his sword hilt and heard him add softly, "And so will I."

Jack continued into a deeper sleep with a peace that was beyond understanding considering the charge he had just been given.

The next morning the group had breakfast and then reconvened in the living room with a beautiful early morning landscape showing in the windows that were not windows.

David smiled at Jack and Laura, "I want you to know that I am really amazed at this fantastic house you call home. I'm sure I don't know the half of it but what I've seen is wonderful. I want one just like it, only in Tel Aviv."

Gary agreed with the Mossad man. "Guys, if I ever win the lottery I want one too. I have never felt more secure and pampered in my life. This beats the best five-star hotel I've ever stayed in by miles. I especially like the baby kitchenette in my bedroom. It's the closest thing I've seen to Star Trek on earth. How does it know how I want my coffee and at what temperature and that I prefer Grapefruit juice to Orange juice? How can it have whatever I want ready, fresh and hot or cold just when I want it? How do the lights modulate themselves so that they fade out when I'm falling asleep and know when to open my window and start my shower in the morning?"

Everyone laughed at the list of questions. Jack answered him, "Gary, it's complicated but I will attempt to explain it when we get a chance. I will tell you that your preferences in the kitchen down here are part of the programming for the unit in your room."

Mark sat back with his cup of coffee in his seat. "Well, where are we in deciding about our course of action? I'm open to any suggestions."

Jack made a little head tilt in Laura's direction and she spoke up. "I think we should go after the NIL and get them off our backs regardless of their super base and host of demons."

Jack sternly looked at Mark. Mark was taken aback at the seriousness of the glance. Jack then voiced his agreement with his wife's decision, "Not only get them off our backs but put them out of business for good. He then told the group the charge and responsibilities he had received from Caleb the night before.

Mark pursed his lips, "How Biblical. The Lord of the Universe has just sentenced the NIL to death by scorched earth policy." He then looked at each of the people in the room, one by one, and asked, "Do you have any problems with obeying Yahveh's commandments to kill every living soul there and destroying everything down to the ground?"

Sensei Grady said, "You realize that the government can't help you in this case? They can't overtly condone a strike into Jordan? We have no real proof, at least not proof they'll accept in a court of law, concerning the upcoming poison to kill children. Even if Caleb were to testify they'd throw it out because he isn't a citizen of a recognized nation."

Mark nodded, "Yes, that's true for overt acts. I'll try to convince the President to help us anyway. He believes in Yahveh, Yahshua, and angels. Who knows? Maybe he can do something."

Everyone considered the risks and problems of that course of action and there was a great deal of discussion about the alternatives and the dangers involved. In the end it was agreed that the team would pull out all the stops, bring in all the favors, and use any means necessary to accomplish the mission. Jack led a prayer of commitment to Yahveh to achieve His goals regardless of the costs to themselves. Ari abstained as an outsider but was willing to do whatever he could to help them against the terrorists.

Then the planning began.

CHAPTER THIRTY-FIVE

Mark punched in the totally secure, private number of the President of the United States. When he was connected directly to the Oval Office he heard the Commander-in-chief of the U.S. ask, "Yes General Connelly, what is the situation?" It was obvious that he was not alone and was probably very busy at the moment. It was an indication of the importance he placed in Mark that he would even take the call in the first place.

Mark answered briefly, "Mr. President, there is a code purple, imminent terroristic threat against the United States and the free world that you need to know about immediately."

The President was silent for a few seconds, "Can you be here at six a.m. tomorrow?"

"Yes Sir" was the answer.

After the connection was broken, Mark called the Air Force base at Colorado Springs and arranged for a quick flight to the nation's capital. This assured that there would be no delays or complications with what weapons he was carrying on his person.

Sarah and David had left for Israel via a special El Al airlines flight over an hour ago. Their trip was to organize the Israeli cabinet of ministers and the Mossad assets for the coming fight.

Jack called a new friend, Victor Chamberlain, now back at his island mansion. "Victor, blessings in the name of Master Yahshua, how is your walk with Him going?"

Victor laughed happily; glad to hear the voice of his new friend. "Fine Jack, I have a church with a pastor and a choir here on the island while I try to learn the basics. Still spiritual milk, but I'm up to milk shakes already and probably ready to try meat in a few weeks. How are you and Laura and the Connelly's?"

Jack had to smile at this new creation in Christ. "We're all well and we need your help with a problem that was the brains behind the people that took over your island. We especially need your financial genius and your nature skills. Could you join us here in Denver and... Oh, bring your credit card."

Victor knew that the request wasn't flippant and he agreed to get there as quickly as he could but he had to wrap up several things first. Hopefully he could be there in time to help them.

Laura began to catalog what the team would need on its trip and started to collect the ordinance. Her organizational talent had always paid off in spades when the chips were down. She concentrated on communications and pulled the Sensei in on this subject. Within two hours they were in downtown Denver meeting with members of the FBI, CIA, and NSA, as well as the Denver Police TACH and SWAT team members. A communication from the office of the President of the United States made it clear that she was to get all of the cooperation they had to give. The complications added by the NIL's overhead satellite observation and communication monitoring were going to be a big challenge.

Gary got with Minister Throman and began to map out the spiritual landmines and traps they could expect with the Muslim radicals and the demonic orchestration. This could well be the most important preparation of the whole mission.

Meanwhile, the enemy was planning its own operation against the American opposition. At the U.S. base for NIL operations in Nevada, it was determined that they were going to have to up the effort level to acquire the third dagger that the Malones most likely had. This time it would be done by serious professionals. The head of the operation felt that the former Russian SPETSNAZ troopers they had hired were more than professionally capable of compromising the home of the Americans and finding anything they were concealing. After the reports from the first team that attacked the house and some building plans he had acquired for a great deal of cash, he was sure the assault would be a success.

The concept of tip-toeing around so that there was no public fuss or police involvement was thrown away during the last try on the Denver freeway. This time he knew that his operation would probably merit international press in its scope and ferocity. He wasn't worried about SWAT teams because he had decided to go with a totally military operation. That was personnel, weapons, and tactics. When he was finished with the Malones they would know that they had been overcome by a superior military force that was unstoppable. He felt that they probably did have the "third dagger" and he actually grinned in anticipation of the carnage to be carried out in the American city of Denver. An Algerian himself, he wanted to bring some war to the Americans.

In a dark place, Astrophel asked a sub-demon, "Are we ready?"

The answer was brief "Yes, exalted one"

Astrophel grinned. His master would be happy with the death and destruction that was about to occur. But even better, he, Astrophel, would finally acquire the crucifixion nail for his master and be rewarded. His laughter was unpleasant.

CHAPTER THIRTY-SIX

Once the military flight to the nation's capital was underway, Mark thought back to his preparations. He had researched every possible method he knew of for attacking the fortified base in Jordan. He had also made provisions to extend U.S. Air Force protection for the El Al flight his wife was on, even if the Israelis didn't know about it. He had set several false leads about both their flight and his to confuse any enemy that might try to interfere with their missions.

Mark recalled his conversation with David and Jack about further attacks against any and all of them. As a result of that brainstorming session he had made a series of calls and requested a variety of help from friends old and new. That should cover that end of things. He felt the summary was ready for the President. As he crossed over Ohio at 40,000 feet and just under Mach 1 he quickly fell asleep.

Jack and Laura were still working on the logistics for their attack on the foreign base when there was a loud blast and a shaking of the house. Jack stood up and Laura went to the weapons locker built into the wall of the den. She brought each of them a .45 caliber pistol and two extra clips of ammo.

Jack saw in the security system at least fifteen men moving towards the house from the north side. They came out of what had been their next door neighbor's pool area. Jack had the odd thought that the Clayton's weren't going to be happy about this. He saw two more men firing shoulder-mounted weapons that looked like RPGs but bigger. There was another big bang and a missile smashed its way through the armor-plated outer wall. Both of the Malones felt the fury of the explosion and sought shelter behind the furniture. Jack knew immediately that the attacking force was using tank buster rounds that could penetrate the armor. This was serious.

As a shower of superheated metal blew into their dining room and melted anything in its path he looked at the .45 in his hand and said to Laura, "I think we're going to need more firepower."

Laura nodded and activated the EWANS system even though both Mark and Sarah were out of the state. She ran for the secure closet on the first floor to get the M-203 combination rifle/.40mm grenade launchers that were stored there. As she ran, a third concussion blew a five-foot hole in the dining room wall and shredded what was left of the polished oak table and chairs. The blast threw her off her feet but she was able to tuck and roll and not get injured in a fall. Her hearing was mostly gone at that point but she was determined to reach the arms locker.

Jack watched as the blast knocked Laura over and bounced him backward. He recovered and took a position to the left of the dining room entrance. A black-suited, helmeted man stepped into the smoking hole holding an AK-47 assault carbine. Jack fired two shots to the face of the helmet because he knew that these troops would be wearing body armor. One shot ricocheted off and hit the ceiling but the second one struck home. The man fell backwards triggering his weapon as he fell. 7.65mm automatic fire chewed up the ceiling and then ceased as death took hold and the already dead man released the trigger in his last fall to earth.

A metal orb sailed through the opening and Jack yelled "Grenade" and dropped to the floor behind a couch and opened his mouth to equalize the pressure. The grenade went off and shrapnel slashed into the walls and furniture. It also knocked out one of the two remaining lights in the dining room.

His head ringing and his vision not too sharp, Jack rolled back to his feet and aimed his handgun at the opening in time to see two more men at the outside of the hole. One of them was aiming a rifle in his direction and there was no time to duck. Bullets passed in mid-flight and smashed into everything but their chosen targets. Then Jack heard a "Ka-chunk" and an explosion blew the two men outside the hole away.

Looking to his right he saw his wife with a smoking grenade launcher and another rifle for him. She tossed it to him and took cover behind the corner of a wall. Jack added another .40mm grenade through the hold to keep them from tossing more grenades into the house and ripped through twenty rounds of .223 caliber ammo for more of the same effect. But he knew that the two of them wouldn't be able to hold off the superior force much longer. It would only take another couple tank-buster rounds and they would have too many fronts to defend. That's if the force outside didn't throw a explosive charge through the hole first.

He was about to motion Laura back towards the safe room when a major explosion lit up the room from outside the hole. Jack crawled back to the den and looked at the picture of the north side of the house. There was a second force out there now and it was decimating the attackers quickly. Jack crawled back to the corner of the dining room and gave Laura a thumb up sign as he yelled at her, "The Marines have landed."

Laura smiled, but with her blast-caused hearing loss she couldn't hear what Jack was saying. She guessed that there was something good going on outside that the attackers hadn't expected, but she didn't have a clue as to what it was.

After several minutes the firing outside tapered off. Then, totally surprising in its innocence after the noise of war, the phone rang. Jack looked at Laura but she still couldn't hear anything. He crawled over to the nearest working phone and answered it. "Hello?"

"General Malone? This is Captain Townsend, U.S. Marine Force Recon. It seems that General Connelly was right in his decision to post us here. We have the situation under control but suggest you stay inside until we can definitely lock down any possible sniper locations. I will call you again when we're sure it is safe."

"Thank you Captain. Who was attacking our house?" Jack was angry, relieved, and spent all at the same time.

"We don't know for sure Sir, but one of my men says that the weapons and tactics are very similar to Russian SPETNAZ troops. I will have a positive ID for you soon Sir. We were able to capture the three wounded that survived."

Jack hung up the phone and put his rifle on safety. He looked around the house and shook his head. Cordite smoke and smoking debris was still everywhere in the air. The north wind from outside the hole in their house was blowing everything around in what was left of the dining room and the hall beyond. The automatic sprinklers had controlled any fire but both the ceiling and walls showed that they had been through a war.

Laura walked over to Jack and shook her head while pointing to her ear. He hugged her and took her away from the damaged area.

After another hour she could hear somewhat and her hearing was improving at a good rate. She thanked Yahveh she hadn't lost her eardrums in the blast.

Captain Townsend and two of his Marines presented themselves at the front door and gave Jack and Laura an update. "Sirs, the enemy has been eliminated and the perimeter is secure. We will continue to keep this area safe but I doubt that they're going to try it here again. We had to kill fourteen of them. Your fire killed three and we captured three. CID is working with the Denver Police to determine who and what these invaders were. The general consensus is that they were once Russian SPETSNAZ troops but they were operating as free-lance on this raid. That's all I have to report at the present." He saluted and both Jack and Laura returned his salute.

The Marines backed an armored personnel carrier up to the north side of the house where the hole had been punched through the outside wall. This effectively sealed off the access until it could be repaired. Jack could see soldiers moving around the perimeter of their house and property in the security scans.

Mark called a few minutes later. "I understand that the Recon was able to help. I hope you guys didn't mind that I arranged for that? I wouldn't want to have spoiled your fun."

Jack replied, "Mark, Yahveh bless you for that. This one wasn't any fun. They were very close to killing us both. If the Marines hadn't come to our rescue NIL would have probably secured the nail by now."

Mark was more sober after that. "I also dispatched a cover force to your dad's church, Larry's home in Dallas, and Minister Throman's home and church. Stay frosty until I get back."

Jack hung up and put his arm around Laura's shoulders. She looked up at him and said, "Now, this is getting too close for comfort."

Jack knew that Yahveh agreed that this had to come to an end. He also knew that he now agreed with Mark about building this home underground.

CHAPTER THIRTY-SEVEN

After his meeting with the President, Mark had all the authority necessary to prepare for any form of attack he wanted to devise. He would have to have the President's approval before he launched such an attack. That was something about another country's sovereign rights. He was on the same USAF plane on the way to Denver to bring everyone up to date.

He looked at the peaceful scene eight miles below his flight and wondered if anyone down there had any clue about the deadly and cruel forces being arrayed against them and their children, mostly for being Christian, free, and successful. He urged the plane on faster in his heart. The attack on Castle Malone had really hit him a lot harder that he let on. He realized that he had taken on the role of protector for Jack and Laura. The fact that the attack came when he wasn't there to help hurt him at levels he didn't know he had when it came to anyone other than his wife. He looked forward to being back there.

High above the earth a rail gun used a series of magnetic pulses to accelerate a two-inch diameter, 5kg, depleted-uranium ball to an incredible 4 kilometer-per-second speed. Aimed by the military electronics and ground computers the ball completed its flight in less than five minutes. At the end of its flight it smashed through an orbiting satellite and the kinetic energy of the ball exploded the satellite into a thousand pieces.

In the darkness below, an almost invisible aircraft was hurtling through the night sky. Already invisible to radar, the warplane held a straight course for its target. The advanced electronics tracked the target and released the bomb at exactly the right time.

The darkness of the pre-dawn hours was ripped to pieces as a new sun appeared. Everyone within four miles of ground zero was killed instantly. The target and the surrounding area where people lived were completely vaporized in an area two miles in diameter and a quarter-mile deep. The flash, heat, and shock waves rolled outward away from the blast site, killing or destroying everything in their path for miles in all directions. The thermonuclear fury died down and all that was left was a huge glowing crater of glass and an expanding fireball of ugly red and black that rose upward for over a mile. Rock formations that had stood for thousands of years and human structures that were brand new collapsed from the shock wave. It didn't matter; there was no life as far as the eye could see in any direction.

After Mark made it back to Denver, he was amazed at the damage sustained and the grim presence of the Recon force surrounding Castle Malone. The Marines had taken some casualties of their own in the previous night's fight and they weren't letting their guard down. The people who lived near Jack and Laura in the up-scale properties in the exclusive neighborhood had probably only seen an Abrams M2 Main Battle Tank on television. Now they had the opportunity for a close look at three of them right in their neighborhood surrounding Jack's house. The Denver Police were doing a good job of controlling the on-lookers. The Marines had added an additional fifty men this morning after the weapons the attackers had brought with them had been analyzed. That many men required a lot of logistics. Some already in place and more were being added by the hour. It would have been impossible to keep a low profile in the neighborhood so they didn't even try.

The Marines, as usual, were being very thorough. Even as General Connelly, Mark had to pass through three checkpoints before being allowed to ask permission of the owners to enter the house.

Laura hugged him more tenderly than ever before. As a combat veteran, Mark knew that a close brush with your own death brings your mortality to mind and that you begin to relish things you had merely acknowledged before. Like friends and comrades-in-arms. He returned the hug just glad that she was all right. He repeated the hug with Jack.

Looking at the damage and dozens of bullet holes in the interior of the house along with the total destruction of the fire-blackened dining room he was sure that Yahveh had protected his friends. He had seen much less damage with much greater civilian casualties around the world when military firepower was used. He thought about his wife in Israel where this type of thing went on all the time. He prayed a sincere prayer in his heart for Yahveh's protection of her.

He sat down and explained his meeting with the President and the reaction to the threat to the children and adults in the non-Muslim world. Then he sobered somewhat, "The President is holding a high-level video conference with the leaders of Britain, Israel, Canada, Mexico, the EU, Russia, China, Australia, and the other countries involved to get their agreement for an attack on the base in Jordan. I don't know what the reaction will be, but the report I gave them was backed up by independent reports from both the British MI-6, and the Mossad as to the reality of this airborne altered-gene, germ-warfare weapon that the NIL has developed. The Mossad provided proof that the weapon or stores of the airborne chemical carrier have already been produced at the Jordanian base and are ready for distribution. I am hoping that the President will be able to persuade the other governments to allow us to be the ones to take down that base. I've done the math. We can do it. It's just that we are going to have to move quickly if we want to prevent them from letting it loose. I think we..."

The ringing of his cell phone stopped Mark in mid-sentence. Flipping it open he said, "General Connelly here." He listened for less than a minute. "Yes, thank you."

Mark hung up the phone and sat there for a few minutes processing whatever he had just gotten over the phone. Then he smiled at Jack. "Well, we can forget raiding the Jordanian base. One of the "non-Muslim extremist countries, and no one seems to know which one. Just dumped a fifty megaton hydrogen bomb on the base and vaporized it completely. That was SatCom with the update. A little over forty minutes ago, every nuclear event warning device they had went off. A fifty megaton hydrogen bomb is a massive explosion. We used to train for reaction to such an attack. Our orders were to cordon off the area and keep people out at a range of thirty miles from the drop zone. There was no reason to go closer".

Jack thought about what Yahveh had commanded. This certainly "killed" everyone and destroyed everything there all right. He asked Mark, "Do you think whoever did this had links to the NIL and were covering their tracks?"

Mark shrugged his shoulders, "No way to tell now."

His cell phone rang again. He listened for quite a while this time. "Okay, thanks." He tipped his head to one side in a thoughtful look. "Every country that has a known presence of the NIL outside of the U.S. has raided them, even Communist Cuba. When the battles were over there were no survivors at any of the sites." Then he added, "Obviously they remember the ASF and the President's demands. At least we won't have to worry about being attacked by these bozos anymore."

Jack wondered about that and asked, "Was there any mention of the NIL presence in Nevada?"

Mark looked at Jack and shook his head. Slapping his hand on the table he jumped up to his feet. "Good point. All right, I think we may have a target after all. And it's not half-way around the world." He headed for the kitchen to make some coffee. This could still be a long night.

CHAPTER THIRTY-EIGHT

Jack knelt in prayer during a lull in the planning of the strike against the NIL group in Nevada. He didn't understand the change in the plans that he thought that Yahveh had given him. He needed to understand what Yahveh wanted him to do. So he prayed, "Dear Heavenly Father, I praise your mighty name and you are worthy to be praised. Father, I'm not sure I understand what has happened. You told me that you were going to give the enemy into my hands but before I could do anything they were utterly destroyed by others. Did I not move fast enough? Did I do something wrong?"

He knelt there in silence waiting for an answer from the Lord, perhaps another visit from Caleb, or Rose. Instead he heard a voice in his mind. *"Oh my son, why do you think you have done wrong? You are preparing for the battle I chose you for. That other place was not for you. Go! And be victorious. I am with you."*

Jack rocked back on his heels and ended his prayer with, "Thank you Father, I pray all things in Yahshua's Mighty Name." He didn't have to test this spirit, he knew the voice of the Father's through His Holy Spirit.

Walking back into the den he called the others together and told them what he had learned. There were quiet agreements with the answer and a rededication to the calling Yahveh had given them. Laura came over and put her hand on his arm, "I'm glad that you asked. I wondered about that too." Jack smiled and kissed her on the forehead.

Even though the NIL had been decimated around the world, David Zahavy returned with Sarah from Israel. "I am glad we don't have to take out the base in Jordan but I remember the discussions about Nevada. I figured you'll still find some way to have some excitement before I have to go home. You know, I'm now not officially here, I'm on vacation."

Mark said, "Excuse me? Did I hear you right? You want to get away from your hum-drum, quiet life in the Mossad to hang around with a bunch of American civilians? WOW! That won't go against you on your next merit review will it?" By the time Mark was finished everyone was laughing. David smiled and replied, "I find this particular group of civilians very unusual, don't you General Connelly?"

Mark was about to retort when his cell phone rang. He answered, "General Connelly." David just smiled.

After the call, Mark called everyone together. There were nine of them now, Jack and Laura, Mark and Sarah, David and Ari, Sensei Grady, Minister Throman, and Gary Eisenthal. Mark held up his hand. "Okay folks, we just got in a "go" command from the President and a load of Intel on this Nevada operation from the alphabet agencies. We need to analyze it as quickly as possible. I doubt that the NIL group will stay there too long. So, Laura, David, Ari, and Gary, I want you to analyze their operation from the Intel from the CIA, FBI, and NSA. Determine what their routines are, where they stay, guard positions, etc. etc.

Sarah, why don't you, Sensei Grady, and Minister Throman work the spiritual and environmental angles from that same Intel. See if there are any terrain features, unique weather patterns, etc. that we can use or that might foul us up. If you see any spiritual problems, highlight them. Jack and I will tackle the satellite and aerial photo recon and see if we can't figure how to bottle the Genie. With that everyone went to work.

Three hours later Jack ran into Mark in the kitchen as they both refreshed their coffee. "Mark, what have you heard about the nuclear strike in Jordan? What's the lowdown on the fallout and collateral damages?"

Mark stopped thinking about the photos and accessed the part of his mind he was using for this particular incident. There were three phone calls and one email. "In summation, well, for starters, the prevailing winds over the strike zone are westerly to south westerly. That means that the fallout from that strike will fall across the desert of Jordan. The only two towns it might strike will be Al Mudawwarah in southern Jordan and Al Bi'r in Saudi Arabia and both of these have been evacuated. The Jordanians are combing the desert along a path that is sixty miles wide for nomads and anyone else in the area.

The scientists that have analyzed the mushroom cloud feel that the bomb was an extremely "clean" bomb and the fallout will dissipate before it goes much farther north, northeast."

Mark paused and took a drink of his coffee.

He smiled at Jack as Laura walked into the kitchen.

"Collateral damage, well, the bomb completely destroyed everything within a twenty mile radius and pretty much flattened everything for another ten miles. But since the base was close to forty miles from anywhere there have been no reported collateral damages other than shaking and light flash."

Jack nodded his head, "Any idea where the bomb came from?"

Mark shook his head. "There was a Stealth fighter, which disappeared from satellite view right after the explosion. That could mean any of twenty different countries. My money is on Russia, China, or even Israel. This type of pre-emptive strike fits their operational profiles."

David walked into the kitchen at that precise moment and overheard the last comments made by Mark. "I can tell you without doubt that it wasn't done by our people."

Mark raised an eyebrow, "Oh, how can you tell for sure? And don't use that old line on me that Israel doesn't have any nuclear weapons."

David was completely serious, "Because we would have used a much bigger bomb, probably a hundred-megaton VDX. We would of done that for three reasons. One, it would ensure no survivability, two, assuming we had nuclear weapons, it would have already been loaded on an aircraft, and three, because if we did have any nuclear weapons we would have more VDXs than any other and you know how frugal we are as a race. But then that would only mean anything if we actually possessed any, which, of course we do not."

Mark looked at the Mossad man for a few seconds, "I think I believe it because of reason one. That is, if you had any, which of course you don't.

Jack smiled at the implications and went back to work.

By four in the morning, everything was complete and everybody crashed for the rest of the short night.

By nine the next morning the planning sessions began.

Mark started the main session by showing a large map of northern Nevada. He indicated the area east of Reno and northward. Then he reduced the coverage to an area of eighty square miles with Winnemucca at the top and bounded by I-80 on the west and state highway 305 on the east. He pointed to a location that was thirty-five miles due south of Winnemucca in the desert.

The next shot was a satellite photo of a complex of five buildings set in the middle of nowhere. Using a graphics package Mark superimposed an overlay over the photo. Then he identified the various structures and outlying areas.

There was a runway to the northeast of the buildings that was pretty well blended into the desert. Building Number 5 was a combination hanger/garage/power generator building. Building 4 was a laboratory/storage space. Buildings 2 and 3 were living quarters for staff and security. Building 1 was the main operations building. Mark pointed at it and stated, "As you can see from this satellite thermal imaging scan there is a complex of tunnels connecting the buildings and several security bunkers around the property. The NSA has identified. machine gun bunkers, here, here, here, and here." As he pointed to circular structures which provided an overlapping field of fire on all sides of the buildings.

Mark then spoke to Jack and Laura specifically as he threw slides up on the screen. "Here are three pictures of the transportation your attackers used to come to Denver before they attacked your house." There were four gray service vans. Each one had a unique rear-view mirror located on the top of the roof near the front. This allowed the driver to keep an eye on the traffic behind him, not just the single car behind him. Each one also had an array of antennas near the back of the van in the middle of the roof. This included a special 18" dish antenna for satellite communications. Black wall tires and Colorado license plates completed the noticeable features of the vans.

"Now," Mark continued. "Here are some satellite photos of our target site in Nevada from three days ago." The pictures showed four boxy vehicles near the main building. Mark zoomed in on the vehicles. There was no doubt that these were the same vans. "So, we've eliminated the possibility that the people at this establishment are just ranchers."

He went back to the overall picture and started detailing how they would take the place and eventually bring it to total ruin as Yahveh wanted. His tactics seemed crazy at first to the other people, but after a few minutes of explanation it became clear that Mark was more genius than nutcase. The plan was brilliant in that it took into account all of the enemy's assets, the available terrain features, time of day, and even the weather.

Everyone started and stared at David Zahavy as he suddenly clapped his hands, applauded, and got up to hug Mark. "If you ever, ever get in the least bit bored, please move to Israel. I will see that you are made a citizen and give you a great position in the Mossad. I have been in combat planning for twenty-five years and what you've done here is absolutely fantastic. It is not at all what I would have done. But then, I would have been wrong. I didn't even see the signs of the land mines you've pointed out. I mean it! Wow!" David walked off praising Yahveh and Mark repeated softly to himself, "No pride, no pride, no pride." He looked up at the others, "Really, this is Yahshua's plan, and I'm only passing it on to you guys."

The only one not enthusiastic about the attack plan was Minister Throman. When Ari saw that he wasn't excited he asked him why not? Alan looked at his new Jewish friend and confided in him. "I'm not sure. There's something not right about this but I can't see what it is. I'm going to fast and pray on this." He excused himself and left for his church.

The rest of the afternoon was packing and preparing the various weapons and making sure their strike was approved by the various federal, state, and local authorities. After an hour or so, Ari tapped Jack on the shoulder. Jack looked up at the only man in the room taller than himself. "Yes Ari, is there something I can do for you?"

Ari seemed somewhat embarrassed but forged ahead anyway. "I don't understand why this particular group of people needs to put themselves in harm's way to do this. Your country has many law-enforcement and military units that are better trained and equipped than we are. I was in combat three times while I served in the Israeli military and am not afraid to participate in this raid. I just need to know, why us?"

Jack asked the Holy Spirit for guidance. "Basically because of the spiritual forces involved. Through His angel Caleb, Yahveh specifically laid this task out for us to do. If we are obedient and do it He said that He would fight for us. The demonic forces involved in this battle are the type that we have come up against several times already in defense of the crucifixion nail. These forces are capable of causing death and destruction unless the people attacking them have the anointing and authorization of Yahshua.

We don't want to be killed or hurt, but if any of the normal police or military units raids this place they will most likely be defeated. Not because they aren't well trained or well equipped, but because they are only going up against the natural, human forces. There are spiritual forces that they aren't prepared for. I don't pretend to understand Yahveh's ideas but then His million-gallon ideas won't fit in my quart-sized mind anyway. I listen, He commands, I obey. The same goes for the rest of the people here."

Jack put his hand on Ari's arm, "Listen, this is what Yahveh told me and through me, the rest of us to do in reference to this enemy." Jack recited the words he had heard from the Father. "*These people who are attacking you are an abomination in My sight. Go up against them and I will give them into your hand. Give ear to my commandments, Utterly destroy all that they are and have, and spare them not; but slay both man and woman, and completely destroy any devices, creations, or efforts they have made. Do all that I say because their evil is beyond belief and will corrupt even the Saints if it endures.*"

Ari didn't know what to believe. He thanked Jack and walked back into the combination living room/den/planning arena. He saw David Zahavy talking with Sarah Connelly and he walked over to them. When they saw the look of concern on his face they asked him what was wrong. Ari looked at his fellow Israeli and said in quiet Hebrew, "I don't know what to make of Mr. Malone and his conviction that he heard directly from Yahveh. I have been going to temple for twenty-three years and I have never even heard of anyone who has heard directly from Yahveh!"

David looked at Sarah and tipped his head to the left. Sarah nodded and walked off into the kitchen. David took Ari by the arm and walked with him into the far side of the living room where there was relatively more peace and quiet. In Hebrew he said, "My friend, let me tell you the story of a dead man that met Yahshua one day."

The discussion went on for quite a while. When they rejoined the group Ari looked at everyone there with a new-found respect and interest. The dead man David was talking about was himself. He had been shot to death in Tel Aviv one day and Laura, Jack, and Sarah had prayed for his life and the Messiah had appeared to the already dead David and told him that He loved him. Touching his wounds the Master had healed him and forever changed the direction of David Zahavy's life. He had not only heard from Elohim but he had met His Son in person.

CHAPTER THIRTY-NINE

The team packed up and left Denver for Reno, Nevada by a MATS (military air transport service) flight at nine p.m. Provided with three Humvees they began the drive to the Nevada NIL base. Each of the team took turns driving and they were in place at the end of the runway at the secret base south of Winnemucca just before 1 a.m. the next morning. After some serious prayer and commitment to Yahveh's will they started the attack, quietly.

Mark, Jack, Laura, and Sarah snuck into the facility and planted explosives and other gear at each of the buildings and the bunkers. They planted ground effects explosives at preselected positions over all the known tunnels and erected an unusual short range launcher near the mine field. They evacuated out of the base and returned to the mobile assault base. They were able to do this without being seen because they had mapped all of the video cameras and view ports and prepared accordingly.

At exactly five a.m. the actual assault began. Detonating the advanced military munitions the team eliminated the firing posts both in the security bunkers and in the buildings. They detonated all the land mines at once through the short launch area explosive that was flung fifty feet above the mine field and detonated. This depressed and released all the triggers at once. The other pre-planted charges took out the hanger/garage/power generation building, the laboratory, and both barracks. The majority of the tunnels were collapsed at the same time as the land mines. The only structure standing after this was the Operations Building.

Wearing full body armor and armed with the latest version of the U.S. Army's combat rifles and optical sights the team quickly eliminated the twelve men who were the remaining defenses for the main building and stormed into the building from front and back simultaneously. Mark's plan was operating at full steam and the enemy personnel had been virtually eliminated before they even realized they had visitors.

Jack and Laura searched the main floors and looked for hideouts and passages to the tunnels. Mark and David cleared the upper floors along with the team of Sarah and Ari. The Sensei and Gary held down the front entrance in the event there were unknown troops or a sudden escape was necessary.

Using the tracking gear the Marines had given them Jack, was able to detect a special passage down from the hall closet that hadn't been seen on the satellite thermal scans. Jack and then Laura tried, unsuccessfully, to reach the other teams by radio. Concerned that the passageway might conceal an active escape path, Jack and Laura moved into the stairway and down three flights to a rock-walled passageway. Figuring they were on a sub level about eighty feet underground Jack reasoned that this was three times deeper than the other tunnels and the reason that it escaped notice. Moving along the wide corridor using their night vision goggles they discovered a set of steel doors that were closed and locked. Jack noticed a camera above the doors and put a bullet through the lens.

Laura fixed a charge to the door and motioned Jack back. She thumbed the remote and the doors left their hinges with a bang. The two of them surged into the large room behind the doors and caught two men trying to burn paperwork on a raised platform that held an altar. Jack triggered a few rounds past their heads to get their attention. Both men grabbed automatic weapons and brought them up to fire. Two streams of 5.56mm bullets shredded the two men where they stood. They didn't even get off one shot.

Jack jumped up onto the platform, pushed one of the bodies aside and flipped up his night vision goggles to see the information on the sheets better. "Looks like battle plans." He shuffled through them and smiled, "Here's one for Castle Malone."

On the first floor, Mark looked around and asked, "Where are Jack and Laura?" No one had noticed their absence up until then. When nobody could contact them or locate them, they searched the first floor carefully.

They had used their Marine detectors but couldn't find any new passageways. Mark started to worry. His cell phone rang and he answered it. It was Minister Throman. "Mark! It's Alan Throman. Don't attack that place!"

Mark asked, "Why not Minister?"

"Because I finally figured out what was bothering me about it. Astrophel and his demons wouldn't die in a nuclear attack. Since all the other bases were destroyed I believe that all the demons would concentrate at that base. The spiritual weight all those demons could bring could cause major trouble for all of you!" Alan was emphatic about needing to hold off the raid.

Mark told him the facts, "We've already completed the attack and have secured the place, but, Jack and Laura have disappeared. Where would these demons most likely be?"

The Minister thought for a few seconds. "They would definitely be below ground. In a cave, or in a basement, something like that, they like the dark. Listen, Victor didn't find anyone at Jack's place so he contacted me. We are headed your way in a VTOL aircraft of his. We should be there in less than an hour."

Mark frowned, "It may be too late by then." Then he hung up. "Okay people, there is a good chance that our missing friends have been suckered by the enemy, probably underground. Let's take this building apart and find that entrance!"

In the subterranean room, Laura noticed it first. A deep chill was seeping into her bones and she didn't like the feeling at all. She was about to say something when a paralysis seemed to have affected her. She couldn't speak, or move. She noticed that Jack seemed to be having the same problem.

Another worldly voice with a very deep register spoke. "Jack Malone, how good of you and your wife to accept my invitation."

Jack was praying furiously in his mind but nothing was happening. All of their weapons were torn away from them by unseen hands and cast aside.

The voice continued, "You see, I knew everything that was going to happen to the misguided human fools that worked for me. But, it was worth it. I now have you where I want you. You need to understand that in this place I am in complete control. No person, not even your God is going to save either of you. I will let you go for a short time to retrieve the crucifixion nail from whatever poor hiding place you have it. If you get back here fast enough I may let your wife live. Do we have an understanding?"

Jack felt the paralysis leave his body. He took off his helmet and threw it to the side. Then he went over to the edge of the platform and sat down.

The deep voice asked, "What do you think you're doing? Do I have to disembowel your wife to convince you that I am capable of doing what I say I am?" A searing pain struck Laura in her midriff, but she couldn't cry out.

Jack had continued praying and was sure of his direction. "No, you don't. I believe you could do it. But it would not change my mind about keeping the nail safe. We've both agreed that we will die for Yahveh to keep the nail safe."

The voice thundered, "Die for Him? You fool! Don't you realize that he is only using you? Would a god that loved you allow you to be put in such peril? Even to costing you the life of your wife? You don't know the real facts about your god. He is a cruel taskmaster that will use you up like cannon fodder and not even be concerned at your pain while you die! I, on the other hand can allow you to reach your true potential. You can be like god. You can rule over the earth if I let you. Your turning the crucifixion nail over to me would assure you of a lofty place. I can offer you any pleasure or fulfill any desire you have. After all I want you to serve me rather than have to hurt your wife."

Jack's eyes went icy-cold. "As my Elohim said to your master in the desert, *"Worship Yahveh and serve him only."* You kill my wife and she will be far better off than the rest of us and it will only serve to make me pity you more." Suddenly he felt the paralysis again. This time it was a crushing paralysis with pain throughout his body.

Laura was released from her stasis. She in turn took off her helmet and then took off the battle armor she had been wearing. She came over and sat down next to Jack. "I don't think you'll have any more success with me than with my husband. And anyway, I don't deal with cowards that are afraid to face me!" She crossed her arms and set her jaw in a statement that was universal sign of stubbornness and rejection.

There was a stirring of the dark and like a curtain being drawn aside dozens of hideous demons came walking, crawling, and flying to surround the two humans. A being of large proportions and ugly as sin stepped forth and paced slowly towards Laura. The demon radiated power and confidence. Fear, lust, and perversion wafted away from him like an aftershave. He stepped up in front of Laura and said, "Do you still think I'm a coward?"

Laura waited for her armor to appear. Nothing happened. Astrophel reached out and ran his massive fingers down the side of her face and neck. Laura felt violated and foul. She wanted to be very afraid. It looked like the demon was right about no one coming to save them. But she remembered Rose's words, "Do not be afraid..." and she let a fire grow in her at this treatment that burned out the fear.

The other demons were crowding in on them now. The stench was horrible. Gnarled fingers and large black claws pulled at both of their clothes and prodded them both.

Laura also remembered that no one had to come to save them. They were already saved. And she also remembered that Yahshua had said that He would be with them. Letting the fire give her courage, she prayed out loud, right into Astrophel's face. "In the name of the Lord Yahshua of Nazareth who came in the..." One of the demons clamped his foul-smelling hand over her mouth, stopping her in mid-word and making her want to vomit.

An evil hiss and the words, "We don't allow that name in here" were followed by a rancid whiff of breath and a tremendous pain in her neck as the demon started pulling her head backwards and down. In seconds she would have a broken neck. Astrophel roared, "No! Let her go you idiot! I will kill her when I am ready, not before!" His huge fist whistled by Laura's head and the demon, the pain, and the hand over her mouth were all ripped off of her and all disappeared at the same time.

One of the demons had a large, ugly knife and was pressing it against Jack's neck. "You want to live? Then admit that your God is impotent and not really interested in what happens to you!" Jack felt fire burning his legs and lower trunk. The smell of burning cloth and flesh was gagging. But the violence just hardened his resolve. He was a child of the most high and these wimps weren't going to convince him of anything else. He struggled against his paralysis hoping to break it.

Laura finished her interrupted statement "...flesh. Master, you said the enemy was under our feet. Help me now Lord."

Astrophel glared at her and threatened to forget his restriction on killing her if she wasn't quiet.

One of the demons was trying to get Laura's shirt off of her but was hindered by the military webbing she was wearing. He pulled and jerked her to the side. Another punch from Astrophel and that problem also disappeared. Laura was buffeted and shaken but noticed an increasing glow behind Astrophel that gave her hope.

Astrophel asked her, "Like I said, do you now think I'm a coward?" He moved right up close to her with the aura of lust overcoming all other sensations.

Laura was quiet for a second, "No, I think you are incredibly stupid!" She started to pray silently. Suddenly a host of heavenly angels appeared around the demons with a great white light that threw everything into stark relief. Astrophel spun around and glared at the angels. "You have no right here!" he thundered.

One of the angels answered him. "The Master of the Universe was asked for help by the young lady there." The angel pointed behind Astrophel at Laura. The demon raised his heavily muscled arm and reached back without looking to grab Laura by the neck, "Well, she isn't asking ever again!" He felt a resistance and turned to look at the woman in glowing gold he was trying to hold onto.

Laura's armor was in full display and she swung the sword of the word with the prayer, *"Yahshua sent them out two by two and gave them authority over evil spirits."* The sword sliced through the arm of Astrophel and knocked him backward.

Rose appeared holding her sword of fire and in one smooth motion cut Astrophel in half. The demon's scream of rage was cut off in the middle and he slowly dissolved into black, oily smoke and disappeared.

Laura saw Rose and the host of angels everywhere battling demons large and small. Laura, screaming her defiance of the evil spirits, charged into the middle of the melee. Swinging her sword left and right she destroyed demons whenever she hit them. Ducking and weaving to avoid the black blades that came at her she continued to wage holy warfare with a continual prayer on her lips.

Jack stood there transfixed. The paralysis was gone but this was not a physical battle. So he began interceding for Laura with the strongest prayers he could make.

The battle ebbed and flowed, first with an influx of more demons that used their greater numbers to gain the upper hand to drive the angels back. But Caleb was always there to encourage and bolster the forces of Yahveh against the forces of evil. One of the largest demons was directing the battle when Laura came up against him. He swung a mighty blow that was stopped by her shield but drove her to her knees. As the demon raised his sword for the finishing blow, Rose's sword sliced him from behind and threw him off balance. He turned and swung at Rose, missing her by inches. He realized his mistake as Laura's sword cleaved him from shoulder to hip. Though fatally wounded, he screamed his defiance until Rose backhanded him with her sword and beheaded him. He dissolved into greasy smoke.

In a flash, the remaining demons fled from the battle, going somewhere with angels right behind them. Laura was left alone except for one of the angels who had fallen where they had been struck down. Laura sheathed her sword and turned to Jack. Her voice was one of compassion and command. "Help me pick him up."

Jack helped her to pick up the fallen angel and carry him to the platform. Once there, they both got down on their knees and Laura thanked Yahveh for the victory and asked Him to tend to his fallen angel.

The quiet in the subterranean room was complete as the angel floated softly up and out of sight. Laura's armor faded and she sagged to the floor. Jack picked her up and headed for the doors and the corridor outside. As he reached the doors he found Mark and the rest of the team standing there armed to the teeth. Ari had been in time to see the end of Astrophel and the battle between the angels and the demons. He watched as two people he had come to respect, as they tended to and prayed for one of the fallen angels. He felt strangely satisfied in his spirit and quite confused in his mind at the same time.

Sarah's face fell as she went to Laura as Jack carried her in his arms. Mark looked at his friends, once again he hadn't been there to help, and smashed his fist against the wall. Jack felt their fear and concern. He smiled, "Don't worry, she'll be all right."

Once they had reached the floor level of the house Jack carried Laura outside and rested her on the bench on the front porch. He checked her vital signs and gave thumbs up for the others. Sarah hugged Mark with relief. Mark continued to watch, waiting to make sure she was all right.

After a few minutes she stirred and tried to sit up. Jack helped her up and held her for long minutes. Mark relieved that she wasn't seriously harmed, got the rest of the team to help him wire the house, the hidden corridor, and the altar room with explosives.

Laura finally stretched and leaned back in Jack's arms. As the rest of the team came out onto the porch she smiled at Jack. "Are we done here?"

"Not quite." Jack led the team in a prayer of thanksgiving and victory in the name of Yahshua.

Jack started walking with Laura down the road to where the truck had been hidden. Just before he got there the rest of the team rushed up and Mark stopped and turned around. He punched the button on the box in his hand and the resultant explosion was more than satisfying to everyone there. There would not be anything for anyone to find. They had done Yahveh's will and utterly destroyed the people and the place.

Just then Victor's VTOL aircraft landed twenty feet away from the truck with the glare of the explosion bright on the glass. Jack and Mark talked it over and split up the team. Jack, Laura, and David were going to go back to

Denver with Victor and the others were going to go back in the truck to Reno.

Laura opened the door to the aircraft. She stopped and looked back at the debris and fire and softly said, "This battle was truly the Master's. Let's go home."

As Mark, Sarah, and the Sensei talked on cell phones to various authorities, Ari pulled the truck onto the two-lane road leading to Highway 305. "I am hoping my Israeli driver's license will work here in America." The VTOL aircraft overflew the truck and wagged its wings as it headed due east. Ari thought about all he had witnessed and that had happened on this trip. This would take a great deal of careful thought and prayer.

The next morning, alone over coffee after a quiet night's rest, Jack asked her, "Honey, what happened in the altar room yesterday?"

Laura thought back and replied, "Yahveh was counting on us to face that demon and help destroy him. Elohim's hands were tied until we prayed for his help. Then he could send all the angels of heaven to our aid, which he did. Astrophel was the power behind all the trouble the NIL was causing. He was doing his master's work and wanted to destroy mankind. The nail would have helped him to do it."

She sighed, "Even with the training you have been giving me I never realized that actual sword fighting was so tiring. I kind of lost it after it was over. But, the Holy Spirit of Yahveh said that we did well."

Jack thought that was high praise indeed. He got up and came around to where Laura was sitting. He knelt down and laid his head on her chest and hugged her tightly. "Telling that demon that it didn't matter if he killed you or not was the hardest thing I ever did." Laura just kept hugging him to her.

Jack leaned back and held her hands. "You realize that it was you that prayed out loud to release Yahveh so he could aid us? I just want you to know that I am so proud of you." Then he grinned, a small grin, "About your sword technique, I think we could work on your stances a little more."

Laura grinned and pushed him over backwards, "Oh yeah?"

CHAPTER FORTY

The weather cooperated and was a beautiful day in Denver for the hot time of year. A cool front had blown down from Canada and the temperature was in the low seventies. The mountains were crystal clear and the soft breezes were like a caress to the skin. The sun was warm but not oppressive as it can be in August even in Denver.

The cook-out had been a great idea to get everybody together without bullets flying everywhere and relax together. Now that the deep ruts caused by the Abrams tanks were repaired, they could again use the large side yard with its beautiful view of the Rockies and Denver.

David Zahavy walked over to where Jack and Laura were standing and asked, "Where is "What's-his-name" and Sarah? And what are all the big tents for?" He was referring to the eight large tents set up on the far side of the yard. The sides were rolled up and the area under the tents provided shade for anyone who wanted it but was definitely overkill for a party with only fifteen people.

Laura answered for them. "Mark and Sarah are out of the country on their company's business. As to the tents, we had arranged for a special lunch for the some of the homeless and the kids of the streets before the attacks by the NIL started. We had to postpone it for a few weeks but we've rescheduled for next weekend. The tents are for games and booths for the kids and lunch for everyone.

David nodded, "That's a great thing to do for people that don't have much of a chance."

Jack added, "We're going to hand out our first run of the LifeCape to them and then see what results they have in four weeks when they are invited back for another lunch."

David looked around at the affluent neighborhood. "Isn't it a little hard for them to get here? And will they be welcome?"

Laura smiled, "We've had three meetings with most of our neighbors and they are all involved and will be here to help serve meals and offer whatever services they can. Several of our next door type neighbors, especially the Monroes have really gotten involved with Jack's "Lord's Lunchbox" and have started similar programs in other cities. She pointed out a couple in their late forties in matching casual slacks and pullovers. "That's Bill and Elaine Monroe, they live right over there." Laura pointed to the north side of their property, "Right past where the two tanks were parked. Bill called over to our place the day after the battle and asked if they could point the cannons a little more to the left because it was scaring their dogs."

The threesome laughed at the picture of the nice suburban couple staring at the business end of two tank cannons.

Jack looked at the Ginger Ale he was sipping on. "Looks like time for more ice cubes. I've had to do some careful public relations to soothe the neighbors and the committee, something about tanks not being in the charter."

David shook his head, "They ought to live in Israel, they'd be glad they live here."

Jack bent down to David's ear and whispered, "We're in the planning stages for a more secure home."

David's eyebrows rose. "More secure? What are you going to do, build it on the moon?" They both laughed at ease with everything going on.

Before Jack could walk back to the bar, Victor Chamberlain walked up to them. "Jack, I haven't had this much fun since I don't know when. You have an amazingly eclectic group of friends and neighbors. And the best part is that no one knows who I am. They just accept me as one of the people, Amazing!"

Laura asked him, "Did you still want to help us next weekend? I would like to show you what wonderful people we met who are on the other end of the financial world."

Victor smiled, "I wouldn't miss it for the world. Neither would Oliver." They all looked at the island native playing chess with the President of a dental software company who was one of Jack's neighbors. It looked like Oliver was winning.

Victor turned somewhat serious and asked all three of them if they could go in the house and discuss some business he was interested in. Jack checked that ever thing was running smoothly and joined the other three in the large family room with the French doors open to the yard.

Victor started off by describing his concept. "Jack, I have studied your LifeCape and its manufacture. I would like to propose a joint venture between your company and mine to distribute the cape along with the food my company makes available to the poor around the world."

Jack thought about that for a minute. It was a wonderful idea but could it work? "I don't know if we have the manufacturing capability to meet such a demand. You know we have planned to sell the LifeCape to the military and the public to secure enough funds to allow us to distribute them free to the needy."

Victor was nodding his head. "Yes, I applaud your generosity but as that chef on TV says, "Let's kick it up a notch." What I am proposing is that Chamberlain Industries foots the bill for a major manufacturing facility to manufacture the cape so that we can get enough of them. I suggest that you keep your Colorado Springs manufacturer running at full speed and we will just add to their output. I realize that I may be horning in on your deal here but I am on fire to do something for Yahshua. This is my chance to really help the people of the world that don't have anything. I am willing to underwrite the entire operation and I'll pay for salaries and raw supplies."

Jack did some quick sums in his head. "I'll tell you what Victor. You give me eighteen million dollars to recoup the development costs that we've already put out and we will call it even. The amount of money brought in from sales of the cape we will split evenly to finance the continued production of the capes. My whole intention for this project was to create something I could give to the people for free. If you want to get on-board then let's do it as a partnership for Yahshua. "

Victor agreed wholeheartedly. He then turned to David. "I would like to suggest that the first distribution of the free LifeCape be in the area around Jerusalem and the Gaza Strip. If Jack and I supply the capes to a "firm" in Israel can you see that they provided them to the needy of those areas?"

David thought about the proposal. "This would be a thing that would help ease Arab-Israeli relations on the grass roots level. I think our government would be inclined to go along with it. At least I can make the suggestion."

Victor shook David's hand. "Let's see what we can do.""Jack, I am using your figures from your manufacture of the capes here in Colorado. It will be at least a year before the new facility will be producing anything. I would like to see if there are any other manufacturers that your company could certify to build the capes until we can come on line. I would really like to get some of these to the people we're providing with food. They really need them."

Jack agreed to seek out other companies to make the LifeCape with the caution that the microelectronic structures required a lot of expensive equipment to manufacture them.

Victor then brought up a problem he had been struggling with for the last few weeks. He looked at all three of his companions. "I am now a born-again, on-fire for Yahshua Christian and I am running head long into trouble with Zarthanians in Zyngola. Can you help me?

Jack looked at Laura and said, "We need to pray about this."

The Crossfire Team returns to new adventures in
"Faith Crossfire".

If this story has awakened you or moved you to seek the love of Christ and His power for your life, whether you've never accepted Jesus as your savior or you've fallen away, repeat the following prayer and begin a most wonderful journey into eternal life with Him today.

Father God in heaven, As You said in Your Holy Word, (Romans 10:9) that if we confess the Lord our God and believe in our hearts that God raised Jesus from the dead, we shall be saved.

(The prayer on the next page is a sample prayer when asking Jesus into your heart as your Savior. You can also pray this in your own words.)

Salvation Prayer

Dear God in heaven, I come to you in the name of Jesus. I confess to You that I am a sinner, and I am sorry for my sins and the life that I have lived; I need your forgiveness. I believe that your only begotten Son Jesus Christ shed His precious blood on the cross at Calvary and died for my sins, and I am now willing to turn from my sin.

Right now I confess Jesus as the Lord of my life and my soul. With all my heart, I truly believe that your Holy Spirit raised Jesus from the dead. Today I accept Jesus Christ as my personal Savior and according to Your Word, right now I am saved.

I thank you Jesus, for your unlimited grace which has saved me from my sins. I thank you Jesus that your grace that never leads to license, but rather it always leads to repentance. Therefore Lord Jesus, transform my life so that I may bring glory and honor to you alone and not to myself.

I thank you Lord Jesus, for dying for me at Calvary and giving me eternal life.

Amen.

If you just said this prayer and you meant it with all your heart, believe that you are now saved and have been born again.

You may ask, "Now that I am saved, what do I do next?" First of all you need to get into a spirit-filled, bible-based church that teaches the Scriptures, and you need to study God's Word.

Once you have found a church home, you will want to become water-baptized. By accepting Christ you are baptized in the spirit, but it is through water-baptism that you publically announce your obedience to the Lord Jesus. Water baptism is a symbol of your salvation from the dead. You were dead but now you live, for Jesus Christ has redeemed you for a price! The price was His atoning death on the cross. May God Bless You!